PHILIP ALLAN
LITERATURE GUIDE
FOR A-LEVEL

DEATH OF A SALESMAN
CERTAIN PRIVATE CONVERSATIONS
IN TWO ACTS AND A REQUIEM

ARTHUR MILLER

Anne Crow

Series editor: Nicola Onyett

PHILIP ALLAN
UPDAT

Philip Allan Updates, an imprint of Hodder Education, an Hachette UK company, Market Place, Deddington, Oxfordshire OX15 0SE

Orders

Bookpoint Ltd, 130 Milton Park, Abingdon, Oxfordshire OX14 4SB
tel: 01235 827827
fax: 01235 400401
e-mail: education@bookpoint.co.uk
Lines are open 9.00 a.m.–5.00 p.m., Monday to Saturday, with a 24-hour message answering service. You can also order through the Philip Allan Updates website: www.philipallan.co.uk

© Anne Crow 2011

ISBN 978-1-4441-2158-2

First printed 2011

Impression number 5 4 3 2

Year 2015 2014 2013 2012

Printed in Spain

Hachette UK's policy is to use papers that are natural, renewable and recyclable products and made from wood grown in sustainable forests. The logging and manufacturing processes are expected to conform to the environmental regulations of the country of origin.

P01811

Cover photo © olly/Fotolia

Contents

Using this guide

Why read this guide?

The purposes of this A-level Literature Guide are to enable you to organise your thoughts and responses to the text, deepen your understanding of key features and aspects and help you to address the particular requirements of examination questions in order to obtain the best possible grade. It will also prove useful to those of you writing a coursework piece on the text as it provides a number of summaries, lists, analyses and references to help with the content and construction of the assignment.

Note that teachers and examiners are seeking above all else evidence of an *informed personal response to the text*. A guide such as this can help you to understand the text and form your own opinions, and it can suggest areas to think about, but it cannot replace your own ideas and responses as an informed and autonomous reader.

Studying a play is different from studying poetry or a novel since it is intended for performance and really comes alive only with an audience. Readers, therefore, must study the stage directions and imagine that they are in a theatre. As a reader, for instance, you might forget about the *'towering, angular shapes'* surrounding Willy's house, but an audience would be oppressed by them in all the sequences located in the present.

Page references in this guide refer to the 1961 Penguin Classics edition of the play (reprinted in 2000). Quotations of stage directions are in *italic*.

How to make the most of this guide

You may find it useful to read sections of this guide when you need them, rather than reading it from start to finish. For example, you may find it helpful to read the *Contexts* section before you start reading the text, or to read the *Act summaries and commentaries* section in conjunction with the text — whether to back up your first reading of it at school or college or to help you revise. The sections relating to the Assessment Objectives will be especially useful in the weeks leading up to the exam.

Key elements

Look at the **Context** boxes to find interesting facts that are relevant to the text.

| Context |

Be exam-ready

Broaden your thinking about the text by answering the questions in the **Pause for thought** boxes. These help you to consider your own opinions in order to develop your skills of criticism and analysis.

Pause for **Thought** ❙❙

Build critical skills

Taking it further boxes suggest plays, websites, films, etc. that provide further background or illuminating parallels to the text.

Taking it **Further** ➤

Where to find out more

Use the **Task** boxes to develop your understanding of the text and test your knowledge of it. Answers for some of the tasks are given online, and do not forget to look online for further self-tests on the text.

Task

Test yourself

Follow up cross-references to the **Top ten quotations** (see pp. 88–91), where each quotation is accompanied by a commentary that shows why it is important.

❮ Top ten *quotation*

Know your text

Don't forget to go online: **www.philipallan.co.uk/literatureguidesonline** where you can find masses of additional resources **free**, including interactive questions, podcasts, exam answers and a glossary.

Synopsis

Top ten **quotation** ❭

The lights come up on a '*small, fragile-seeming home*', which is constructed so that the audience can see simultaneously the kitchen and the two bedrooms and so that the actors can walk through the walls in Willy's imagined memories. The house is surrounded by '*towering, angular shapes*', and the accompanying music, played on a flute, '*is small and fine, telling of grass and trees and the horizon*'. As the audience tries to reconcile these contrasting moods, Willy Loman, an ageing and exhausted salesman, carries his cases across the stage and into the house where he is greeted by his loving wife, Linda. He has returned unexpectedly, having failed to reach his territory in New England, and he is confused because he was unable to concentrate on driving.

We guess from the title of the play that he will die, and Miller focuses on the last 24 hours of his life, gradually revealing how he has been brought to this point. Through conversations and scenes that take place in Willy's mind, Miller reveals Willy's hopes, dreams and secrets as well as the truth behind them. The play is a psychological drama and the audience is invited to see inside Willy's mind and to try to understand why it is disintegrating to the point where the only way he can see of fulfilling his dream is to commit suicide.

Willy's father sold home-made flutes as he travelled west with his family, but he deserted them when Willy was three, and went to Alaska. Willy never recovered from this abandonment. His older brother, Ben, also left when he was 17, going to Africa, where he worked in the diamond mines and became rich. Willy started working as a travelling salesman while still a teenager. Ben visited Willy once, offering him a job in Alaska, but Willy had met an elderly salesman who was able to drum up business by phone and whose funeral was attended by hundreds of salesmen and buyers. This dream of popularity and commercial success was stronger than his drive for adventure and the great outdoors, so he declined Ben's offer, a decision he now regrets.

Willy opened up new territories for the Wagner company, but was never very successful and, in a rare moment of truth, admits that people do not take to him. Nevertheless, he and Linda have just paid off the mortgage on the house in Brooklyn, a borough of New York. When they bought it, 25 years earlier, they had a lovely garden and hung a swing on adjoining land between two large elm trees. The trees were cut down to make room for '*a solid vault of apartment houses*', which overshadows

Context

In 1947, Miller said, 'In all my plays and books I try to take settings and dramatic situations from life which involve real questions of right and wrong.'

Context

In 1925, President Calvin Coolidge said, 'the chief business of the American people is business. They are profoundly concerned with buying, selling, investing and prospering in the world.'

Top ten **quotation** ❭

the garden, so nothing will grow. Willy pinned all his hopes on their firstborn son, Biff, who was successful at sport, popular at school and had scholarships to three universities.

Willy, however, had taught Biff that being well-liked was more important than studying, so Biff often skipped maths lessons to play football, relying on Bernard, the hard-working boy next door, to tell him the answers. Biff was captain of the football team and, just after a prestigious match, he learned that he had failed an important maths exam and so would be unable to graduate. Biff idolised his father so he travelled up to Boston to ask Willy to talk to his teacher, convinced that Willy would be able to persuade the teacher to give him the extra marks.

Biff's world was shattered because he found his father with another woman. He dropped out of school, spent six or seven years trying to work himself up in various businesses and then, before the Second World War, left home and went west, working as a farmhand. Willy has repressed the memory of Biff's visit and refuses to accept responsibility for Biff's failure, thinking he is acting out of spite. They argue whenever they are together.

When the play opens, Willy has been taken off his salary and is earning only commission, so he has to borrow money from Charley, his successful neighbour. He has 'cracked up' at work at least once; he has had several non-accidental car crashes, and there is evidence that he is thinking of gassing himself. Biff has told his father of big plans for the future, but he needs capital to set up the business. Willy feels a failure; he cannot even grow seeds to invest in the future. However, he does have an insurance policy and, when he goes off-stage to kill himself, he is imagining Biff's success when he has $20,000 in his pocket.

> **Context**
>
> The Brooklyn Navy Yard brought thousands of workers to the borough during the two World Wars, and new subway lines built in the 1930s made it easy to commute between Brooklyn and Manhattan.

Act summaries and commentaries

The action of each act is seamless, but I have created divisions to facilitate study. In the *Michigan Quarterly Review,* 1985, Miller wrote:

> **The form of *Death of a Salesman* was an attempt, as much as anything else, to convey the bending of time. There are two or three sorts of time in that play. One is social time; one is psychic time, the way we remember things; and the third one is the sense of time created by the play and shared by the audience...The play is taking place in the Greek unity of 24 hours; and yet it is dealing with material that goes back probably 25 years. And it almost goes forward through Ben, who is dead. So *time* was an obsession for me at the moment, and I wanted a way of presenting it so that it became the *fiber* of the play, rather than being something that somebody comments about.**

The summaries in this section have been organised in two columns. The left-hand column describes events in 'psychic time', as they are replayed in Willy Loman's memory or imagined by him; the right-hand column describes events in the present, or 'social time'.

Context

Miller said, 'in the theater you can sense the reaction of your fellow citizens along with your own reactions. You may learn something about yourself, but sharing it with others brings a certain relief — the feeling that you are not alone; you're part of the human race' (*The Sunday Times*, 3 November 1991).

Act One, pp. 7–13

Psychic time	Social time
Flute music tells of '*grass and trees and the horizon*'.	
	'*Towering, angular shapes*' and '*an angry glow of orange*' suggest a feeling of claustrophobia and frustration.
	Willy, an ageing salesman, returns home and is greeted by his wife, Linda, who is worried about him. She urges him to ask for a job in New York. Biff, their son, and Willy had had a row that morning. Willy remembers how popular Biff was at school. He remembers elm trees, swing, flowers — now he feels boxed in.
	Biff and Happy, the younger son, listen. Willy resolves to leave Biff alone. He remembers the Chevrolet and Biff simonizing it. He goes down to the living room, mumbling about the car, and Linda, clearly worried about him, walks out.

Commentary: **The title of the play suggests that Willy defines himself by his job, rather than by his private persona as a** husband and father. This foreshadows his death as soon as his job has been taken away from him. Of course, the title may also refer to Dave Singleman, who died the death of a salesman. This death symbolises Willy's dream of success, as hundreds of salesmen and buyers were at his funeral.

Willy '*thankfully lets his burden down*'. We are never told what is in the suitcases, but Miller's choice of word is reminiscent of Christian in Bunyan's *The Pilgrim's Progress*, who also carried a 'burden', the knowledge of his own sin. Symbolically the cases seem to contain a lifetime of cares and worries, but Miller has also subtly suggested Willy's preoccupation with past mistakes.

Taking it **Further** ➤

Check out a photograph of an apartment building in Brooklyn, taken about 1940, on www.museumoffamilyhistory.com and go to Site Map / Memories of my Family / A Family Portrait: a Childhood of Memories

Context

Miller wrote 'I've come out of the playwriting tradition which is Greek and Ibsen where the past is the burden of man and it's got to be placed on the stage so he can grapple with it' (*Arthur Miller And Company*).

John Springer Collection/Corbis

Willy (Fredric March) returns home, in the 1951 film version of the play

Linda's '*trepidation*' signals that she fears something is wrong, but Willy reassures her with a declarative statement, 'I came back', which hints that he might not have done. Linda speaks '*very carefully, delicately*', and we are aware of some unspoken tension. Miller gives Linda lines that raise our expectations and suggest how the play will develop. She seems to have expected him to 'smash the car', and she begs him to ask his boss for a job in New York. This interview does not take place until the second act, but Miller makes us aware of its importance from the start.

Taking it **Further** ➤

Watch an amusing film of driving around New York in 1928. Go to www.youtube.com and search for 'Driving around New York city 1928'.

Linda knows Willy is suicidal, that his mind is disintegrating, and she does all a lay person can do to keep him in touch with reality. She gives him excuses (the steering, his glasses), and she offers simplistic solutions like an aspirin to give him some hope. She takes off his shoes, not because she is the stereotypical downtrodden wife, but because he is precious to her, and she does everything she can to ease his burden and make him feel more confident with himself. Miller wrote: 'It's very important to understand that Linda is aware of the real story from the moment the curtain goes up. She knows Willy is suicidal, and when you're living with a suicidal person, you tread very carefully' (*Michigan Quarterly Review*, 1998).

Willy thinks it ironic that you 'work a lifetime to pay off a house. You finally own it, and there's nobody to live in it'. He wants to keep hold of the past and still have his sons living at home. Linda is more pragmatic and knows that it is natural for children to move on. The irony is that Willy feels that he has not accomplished anything, even though they are about to pay the last instalment on the house. Willy's dream of accomplishing something spectacular makes him dissatisfied with what he has achieved. He views success in terms of money, so he judges Biff by the amount he earns and places no value on the fact that Biff is living the life he loves and, ironically, the life in the open air that Willy himself would have preferred.

Willy often seems to contradict himself because he is unable to articulate his thoughts. When he says that Biff is a lazy bum, he is complaining that Biff has no ambition for material success rather than that he shuns hard work. Gradually, we are becoming aware that Willy subscribes to the contemporary interpretation of the American Dream and believes that 'personal attractiveness' and hard work are enough to guarantee financial success.

Linda tries to bring Willy out of his reminiscences and keep him in touch with the present by suggesting he try the new cheese. Miller has told us that she is '*most often jovial*', and her superficial laugh here suggests that she may have bought whipped cheese deliberately for an occasion like this, knowing that his irritation with the present would prevent his mind from sliding backwards.

Context

Dale Carnegie's self-help book, *How to Win Friends and Influence People,* was published in 1936 and sold 30 million copies. It draws in part on lessons the author learned working as a salesman for Armour.

Act One, pp. 14–21

Psychic time	Social time
Willy mumbles to himself.	
	Biff and Happy discuss Willy's driving, the old times, dreams and plans, women. Biff wonders why Willy mocks him all the time. Happy tells him Willy talks to himself, mostly about Biff. Biff is working in Texas; he likes the open life but every spring feels that his life has been wasted. Happy has a steady office job, but pretends he is an important executive. He is attractive to women and steals the girlfriends of his superiors, but he is lonely. He wants to meet somebody with character, like his mother. The brothers discuss building a business together out west, but Happy wants to prove himself in New York first. Biff thinks of borrowing money from his former employer, hoping that he will not remember the stolen basketballs.
Willy's mumbling becomes audible again.	
There is a long overlap between this scene and the next as we hear Willy talking to Biff as he polishes the car.	Biff is annoyed at Willy because his mother can hear. Happy tells him to sleep.

Commentary: **Biff and Happy are alone together after a year's separation, so they can talk frankly, and Miller is able to give the audience some background information. The theme of sexual relationships, which will become very important as we learn about the woman in Boston, is introduced here, and we learn that Biff has become more 'bashful' and Happy less so. Miller hints that something has happened to knock Biff's confidence, and it seems to have something to do with Willy. Miller tells us that both men are '*lost*'. Biff is unhappy that his father mocks him and that he cannot get near him. He hints that he knows something about why Willy is depressed.**

Neither Linda nor Willy has spoken of Willy's previous car crashes, although both will have been thinking of them. Miller uses Happy to impart this information. Happy is worried about Willy, but Biff, who has been away for a long time, seems unconcerned, suggesting facile reasons for his behaviour. Gradually, his resentment surfaces, and there are various hints that something unspoken lies between Biff and Willy.

We become aware that Biff is similar to Willy in being torn between the desire to achieve success in the modern world and a longing for open spaces and a connection with the land. Biff has inherited his grandfather's wanderlust and his father's puritan belief in not wasting your talents.

Context

In *Salesman in Beijing,* Miller explained that Biff has returned home 'to somehow resolve this conflict with [his] father, to get his blessing, to be able to cast off his heavy hand and free [him]self' (Methuen, 1983).

Happy's dream of being merchandise manager and having 'the waves part in front of him' when he walks into the store, is similar to Willy's dream of being like Dave Singleman. Even if he were to achieve this, it would bring him no satisfaction — like the present manager, he would keep dreaming of something bigger and better. Happy has inherited his father's competitive nature, which manifests itself in his compulsive seduction of the fiancées of executives of his firm. He laughs but despises himself. The conflicting values with which he was brought up are revealed in the puritanical way he speaks of the girls as 'ruined' because he has slept with them. He takes bribes, but hates himself for it, believing himself essentially honest. His 'over-developed sense of competition' means that he takes whatever he can get and loves it.

Linda has provided a model for Happy to look for in a wife. She is 'somebody with character, with resistance'. Biff clearly admires her too, and his anger at Willy is because his mother can hear what Willy is muttering. He begins to get angry because Willy '*laughs warmly*', a hint that foreshadows the disclosure of the fatal secret.

Act One, pp. 21–32

Psychic time	Social time
	Willy enters the kitchen. Gradually the house and its surroundings become covered with leaves, indicating that, inside Willy's head, he is in the past.
Willy is giving Biff advice about girls.	Willy pours milk.
Willy is happy, smiling broadly and laughing, as he talks to the boys about cleaning the car and hanging a hammock.	
Biff and Happy come in as schoolboys, clearly adoring their father. Willy gives them a punchbag. Biff shows a ball he 'borrowed' from the locker room and boasts about how the coach praises him. Willy seems jealous of his neighbour, Charley, who, he says, is not well liked. Willy boasts that one day he will have a bigger business than Charley's. He boasts of his successes and promises the boys they can accompany him in the summer.	
Biff is the centre of Willy's attention: twice Happy tries to get noticed by lying down on his back, pedalling in the air and declaring that he is losing weight.	
Bernard comes in saying that if Biff does not study he will fail the Regents exam, even though he has scholarships to three universities. Willy tells the boys that looks and personality are what matter.	

Linda enters. The boys carry the washing for her. Willy lies to her about how much commission he has earned. He is not earning enough to cover their payments on the mortgage, washing machine, vacuum cleaner as well as repairs to car and house. Willy admits to Linda that people do not like him. They laugh at him and respect Charley. Linda reassures Willy. He tells her he gets lonely on the road and worries he will never achieve his dreams.

Embedded within this remembered scene is a dramatised memory of the woman thanking Willy for the stockings. She boosts his ego, makes him feel liked.

As the light fades on this scene, it brightens on the kitchen, revealing Linda mending stockings. Feeling guilty, Willy gets angry with her, insisting she throws them out.

Bernard, Charley's son, enters. He cannot give Biff the answers on a state exam and Biff is driving without a licence. Linda worries about Biff taking the football and about how rough he is with the girls — all the mothers are afraid of him.

The woman is heard laughing.

Willy explodes in anger and defends Biff.

Back in the present, Willy wonders why Biff is stealing and deludes himself in not accepting responsibility.

Commentary: **As Willy's reminiscences take over, his voice gradually rises from a mumble to that of a normal conversation. He seems to be remembering a conversation he had with his sons, but we cannot tell how far it is a real memory and how far an imagined one. He seems to be confusing two memories, one of 1928, in which he gives the boys the punchbag with Gene Tunney's signature, and one of Biff's graduation in 1932.**

Willy's advice to Biff not to get too serious with girls is ironic after the earlier conversation between Biff and Happy, and in the light of Willy's own infidelity, which is suggested in this scene. Although Willy gives Biff good advice to 'watch your schooling' and to return the stolen ball, he actually encourages the boy's dishonesty by *'laughing with him at the theft'* and by excusing his behaviour. He is teaching Biff that he is special, that he can get away with breaking the rules, if he is well liked. He encourages Biff to take off his helmet and break through for a touchdown, even though the coach has obviously told him to pass the ball.

Context

James Joseph 'Gene' Tunney was world heavyweight boxing champion from 1926 to 1928 and retired as an undefeated heavyweight after his victory over Tom Heeney in 1928.

Willy with Biff and Happy as boys, from the television film version of 2000

AF archive/Alamy

Context

The Regents are exams set by the New York State Education Department for high-potential students. Like A-levels, they are administered according to strict and specific instructions, with no opportunity to cheat.

*Pause for **Thought*** ⏸

Do you think Willy really hit the salesman or is this how he thinks he ought to have reacted? Either way he was clearly unstable and vulnerable then.

Willy boasts to the boys, and he is clearly embellishing the facts, claiming to have had coffee with the mayor of Providence and that the police protect his car. This suggests that he feels inadequate: he needs to impress his sons and fears that the truth would not do so. He also encourages the boys to despise the '*earnest and loyal*' Bernard, to whom he is very rude: 'What an anaemic!' Willy really believes that his sons' looks will take them further than Bernard's hard work.

In Willy's memories, Linda is always working, carrying washing, waxing floors or mending stockings. Gradually, his inflated ego calms down in Linda's presence. She never falters in her appreciation of him when he changes his figures from 1,200 gross to roughly 200. '*Without hesitation*', she works out the revised commission and tells him it is 'very good', even though it is not enough to pay the bills.

Even in his forties, Willy's personality was volatile: he tells Linda of an incident when, just as he was going in to see a buyer, another salesman apparently called him a walrus and Willy 'cracked him right across the face'.

In Willy's memory, Linda tries to cheer him by telling him he is the handsomest man in the world. This triggers a memory of the woman, who tells him he is wonderful. He has '*massive dreams*' of building 'a business, a business for the boys' and, as he speaks of what he wants to make for them, the word 'make' becomes part of his embedded memory of the woman. She uses 'make' as a slang term for picking up a woman for sex. We can dimly see her getting dressed, so the implication is obvious. However, there is no talk of love, so we realise that she is no threat to Linda.

The woman thanks him for the stockings and, as he emerges from this embedded memory into the same reminiscence as before, the woman's laughter ironically blends into Linda's as she laughs at his protestation that she is the 'best there is'. Willy sees Linda mending stockings, which have become a symbol of his infidelity and his shame. He angrily orders Linda to throw them out but, instead of obeying him, she quietly puts them in her pocket to mend another time.

Now that Willy's happy reminiscence has become contaminated by his feelings of guilt, all the complaints about Biff start to harass him at once. We hear the woman laugh again, and Willy says 'Shut up!' but it is not clear whether he is speaking to the woman or to Linda and Bernard. He becomes increasingly agitated until he explodes at Linda, who retreats in tears. Linda does try to influence the way Willy is bringing Biff up but Willy is absolutely convinced he is right, and Linda has succeeded only in making him lose his temper.

As the leaves fade, the apartment houses once again dominate the stage and Willy comes back to the present, but he is still thinking in the past, and we realise that he is defending himself against taking the blame for Biff's dishonesty.

Act One, pp. 32–41

Psychic time	Social time
	Happy comes downstairs, concerned for Willy. Willy stops speaking of Biff and voices worries about Linda. He regrets not going to Alaska with his brother, Ben.
	Charley enters. Happy goes back to bed. Charley and Willy play cards. Charley offers Willy a job, but Willy is insulted.
	Totally oblivious to Charley's evident concern, he asks, 'What do you keep comin' here for?' Willy wonders why Biff is going back to Texas.
Ben enters and inspects everything. He tells Willy he is looking at properties in Alaska.	Charley briefly recalls him to the present and Willy tells him that Ben died in Africa, and he had seven sons. Ben was the only man Willy knew with all the answers.

Willy starts to answer Ben, telling him that their mother died a long time ago.

Willy asks Ben for the answer. Linda enters and speaks to Ben, but Willy pulls him away impatiently. He asks Ben about their father. Ben also left home, went to diamond mines in Africa and made his fortune. Willy introduces him to Biff and Happy. Ben tells them that his father was a 'Great inventor' and very successful.

Willy sends the boys to steal sand from a building site. Charley enters and warns Willy about the police. Bernard enters, saying the watchman is chasing Biff.

Willy feels 'temporary' about himself because his father abandoned him when he was so young. Willy longs for Ben's support. Ben walks out, reinforcing Willy's belief that courage will make a man rich.

For a while, Willy hovers on the brink between illusion and reality. Charley hears only Willy's side of the conversation and is confused. Willy is 'unnerved' by his own confusion and unable to concentrate on the game. He accuses Charley of cheating. Charley's patience is exhausted as he realises that he cannot help. He leaves.

Willy is still speaking to Ben when Linda comes down, concerned about him. When Ben visited, he gave Willy a diamond watch fob, but Linda reminds him he pawned it to pay for a course for Biff. Willy goes out in his slippers.

Commentary: **Willy does not own up to Happy that he could not concentrate on driving, as that would betray weakness. Instead he says that he nearly hit a child. Is this the truth or an attempt to save face by giving a more manly reason for his premature return?**

Charley speaks with '*pity*' and '*trepidation*'. Like Linda, he also realises that Willy is suicidal and tries to handle Willy by not antagonising him. He takes no offence at Willy's insults, tries to distract Willy with a game of cards, and encourages him to talk about things he is good at.

When Charley tells him to forget Biff, Willy poignantly says, 'Then what have I got to remember?' In Willy's estimation, he has achieved nothing in his life, and all his hopes are now centred on his son. Willy is proud of the improvements he has made to the house and despises Charley for not being capable with his hands, but these achievements do not fulfil his dreams, so he remembers the one opportunity he had to get rich, and he starts talking to Ben. This is the first time in the play that the real world becomes confused in Willy's mind with the world of his memory and imagination. Even in a single response, Willy is talking to both characters, first Ben then Charley: 'Long ago. Since the beginning you never knew how to play cards.'

Willy is remembering a time when he was in his forties, but Miller describes Ben as '*in his sixties*', which suggests that Miller intended him to be a figment of Willy's imagination rather than a memory. In Willy's imagination, Ben is always in a hurry, chasing opportunities to make more money. Miller shows us that Ben has achieved success at the price of abandoning his mother and younger brother, and cutting himself off from his family. He does not even know that his mother died 'a long time ago'. Ben speaks '*with a certain vicious audacity*' and, when Charley warns Willy that 'the jails are full of fearless characters' who have committed theft, Ben adds 'And the stock exchange', which is a telling criticism of capitalism.

In Willy's imagination, Ben also makes hyperbolic claims, saying that, by selling his home-made flutes, their father 'made more in a week than a man like [Willy] could make in a lifetime.' Ben encourages Biff to fight, in spite of Linda's remonstrance, and teaches him 'never fight fair with a stranger'. Linda is frightened by this and is cold towards him, apparently realising that Ben's arrival is going to have a detrimental effect on Willy.

As Ben laughs at Charley, Willy joins in, but his laughter rings hollow as his worries about Biff stealing are surfacing in his mind. Willy is remembering a period during the 1930s' depression when business was bad for everyone, but he refuses to admit that times are hard. Charley's sarcasm indicates that he knows Willy is lying. Nevertheless, Willy did weather the depression, and kept up the payments on his mortgage and appliances, which was quite an achievement. In Willy's imagination, Ben approves of the way he is bringing the boys up, but we cannot tell whether this is a genuine memory or a wish-fulfilment dream.

> **Context**
>
> The Wall Street Crash of 1929 followed a speculative boom that had taken hold in the 1920s. This led hundreds of thousands of Americans to invest heavily in the stock market, a significant number even borrowing money to buy more stock.

Act One, pp. 41–54

Psychic time	Social time
	Biff enters, swearing. Linda defends Willy against Biff's criticism: Willy is 63 and exhausted; his company has taken his salary away; he borrows money from Charley and pretends it is his wages. Biff says they fight because he knows his father is a fake, but refuses to explain.
	Finally, she attacks both sons for their neglect and reveals that Willy's salary has been taken away. Biff reluctantly agrees to stay but Linda is not satisfied. Willy needs emotional support so she details his suicide attempts and collapses into tears, which reduces Biff to '*a fever of self-reproach*'.

Biff and Happy argue. Biff says the family does not belong in a city. Willy enters. He heard Biff say that the business world laughs at him, and is angry. He stresses his popularity. Happy tells Willy that Biff is going to see Oliver, and Willy's mood immediately changes to one of optimism until he realises nothing is definite. Biff and Willy argue. Happy stops them with the plan for a partnership. The whole family is wildly enthusiastic.

Willy gives Biff advice, cutting Linda out when she speaks. There is another argument as Biff defends Linda. Willy, '*suddenly beaten down, guilt ridden*', goes out. Linda rebukes Biff, asks him to say goodnight to Willy and then leaves.

Biff and Happy talk then go up to their parents' bedroom. Willy cannot resist giving advice. Biff cannot bear it and walks out. Happy tries to get attention.

Willy remembers the Ebbets Field game and Biff's popularity and success. Linda asks what Biff has against him — no answer.

Biff goes down to the kitchen and, '*horrified*', removes the rubber tubing.

Commentary: **Linda unsuccessfully employs feminine wiles to arouse Biff's sensitivity, using emotional blackmail and the '*threat of tears*', then she resorts to a direct and impassioned plea that people like Willy should not be ignored. Reluctantly, she has to confide in them the painful truth and that she does not know what to do.**

Miller drops a lot of hints that Biff knows something about Willy that he refuses to share. He is evasive when Linda asks for explanation. He declares that Willy is a fake and refuses to explain, and he picks up on Linda's mention of a woman, '*sharply but contained*', asking, 'What woman?'

Willy has contradictory views of his father. Ben makes extravagant claims that suggest that Willy admires his father as a pioneer, an inventor and a salesman. Here, however, he walks in saying, 'Even your grandfather was better than a carpenter.' The intensifier 'even' shows that Willy does not value skilled craftsmen. He asks Biff, 'Go back to the West?' and contemptuously defines this as 'Be a carpenter, a cowboy, enjoy yourself!'

Willy gives Biff contradictory advice; he says, 'Be quiet, fine, and serious' then 'Walk in with a big laugh. Don't look worried. Start off with a couple of your good stories to lighten things up.' In spite of all his years in the job, Willy is still unsure of the best way to approach people.

If we hear just the spoken words, the first act seems to end in a mood of optimism. Willy is confident that Biff will 'be great yet', and he plans to ask for a New York job. After remembering Biff as the golden boy ('Like a young god. Hercules'), he

Context

Until the whole country had been explored and inhabited, the West was the symbol of opportunity but, by the twentieth century, the Eastern Seaboard was where challenges were to be found, and businesses flourished that held promises of wealth.

Context

In Roman mythology, Hercules was a demi-god, son of Zeus, famed for his strength.

PHILIP ALLAN LITERATURE GUIDE **FOR A-LEVEL**

watches the romantic symbol of the moon, which is not quite obscured by the buildings. The stage directions, however, tell a different story. The light on Willy and Linda's bedroom fades so that the audience's attention is drawn to the gas heater. This reminds the audience of Willy's suicidal thoughts. Biff stares at the heater, reaches behind it and removes the tubing, '*horrified*'. This suggests that he has accepted responsibility for his father. As Willy talks hopefully of the next day, Linda starts humming a soft lullaby to relax him. Gradually this humming becomes '*desperate but monotonous*', creating an ominous mood of fear.

*Task **1***

At the end of Act One, what seem to be the reasons for Willy's attempts to commit suicide?

Act Two pp. 55–59

Psychic time	Social time
	Next morning, Willy is happy and hopeful, thinking of growing vegetables. He starts to dream of buying a place in the country.
	Because he is happy and optimistic, Linda is '*joyful*', but she is more practical: she struggles to get him into his jacket, button it up as he unbuttons it, and to make sure he has his glasses and a handkerchief.
	He is determined about his interview with Howard. Linda reminds him how much money he needs to ask for as an advance and then tells him of the dinner arrangement with his sons. The stocking in Linda's hand makes him nervous.
	Biff rings. Linda is disappointed to learn that it was Biff who took away the tube. She tells him Willy is in high spirits and tells Biff to be loving.

Commentary: **Linda helps Willy to get dressed as if he is a child on his first day of school, reminding the audience how much he relies on her. As she tries to get him into his jacket, he walks away then unbuttons it, actions suggesting that he would be more comfortable in his shirt-sleeves working out of doors. The tragic irony is that Willy's new dream is achievable: they could sell the house in Brooklyn and buy a little place in the country and be self-sufficient, but Willy is used to living in dreams and does not ever translate them into reality.**

Willy's complaint that he is 'always in a race with the junkyard' strikes a chord with anyone who has bought an appliance through hire purchase, but this scheme has allowed Willy and Linda to have modern conveniences like a refrigerator and a vacuum cleaner, without having to save up for them. However, the free availability of credit has meant that they have over-reached themselves and are struggling to meet all

Context

Hire purchase was first used to sell household goods to low-income families. After 1916, when manufacturers began to offer cars on time-payment plans, hire purchase was extended to include household appliances that otherwise would have been out of reach for the average family.

grace period

Extra time allowed by an insurance provider for payments to be made without penalty.

the repayments. Miller slips in the first reference to the life insurance that is to become so significant, as Linda reminds Willy that they are already into the *grace period*. Willy's optimistic mood is clouded by guilt at the sight of the stocking as he goes off to see Howard.

Act Two pp. 59–66

Psychic time	Social time
	Willy approaches Howard in his office. Howard is playing with a new gadget, a wire-recording machine, and takes little notice of Willy. Suddenly, he realises something must have happened and asks Willy why he is not in Boston. Willy asks for a job in town and gradually, desperately, reduces the amount he is asking for. He talks to Howard about the past: his own father, Dave Singleman, Howard's father, but Howard is interested only in the present. Willy becomes desperate and starts '*banging his hand on the desk*' and '*yelling at him*', so Howard makes an excuse and leaves the room.
Willy drifts into the past, looking at Howard's chair but talking to his old boss.	Accidentally, Willy turns on the machine and panics, frightened by the sudden noise. Howard returns and tells Willy that he cannot represent the company any longer. He tells Willy to look to his sons for support. Willy stares into space, exhausted.

Commentary: **Unlike the advice he gave to Biff, Willy is humble towards Howard and tries to please him by showing appreciation of Howard's children and of the wire-recording machine. In an effort to appear confident, he pretends that he will buy a machine and that he has a car radio. Howard knows that Willy has 'cracked up' before, and, when Willy becomes angry and desperate, it becomes obvious to Howard that Willy is no longer able to cope. His irrational behaviour when the machine starts up prompts Howard to gently advise a 'rest'. However, he mitigates his action by leaving the possibility open that he might find something for Willy once he has had 'a good long rest'.**

Howard contradicts Willy's claim that he averaged $170 a week in 1928, reinforcing our impression that Willy has exaggerated his success with the Wagner Company.

Willy makes a long speech about Dave Singleman, who died the death of a salesman in a railway carriage on the way to his territory at the age of 84, never having earned enough to retire. Willy is impressed that 'hundreds of salesmen and buyers' were at the funeral, but he does not mention family. Either Singleman had none or Willy rates success only in terms of his job.

Act Two pp. 66–71

Psychic time	Social time
Ben enters. Willy confesses that 'nothing's working out' and asks him for the answer. Ben asks Willy to go to Alaska. Willy is enthusiastic but Linda reminds him that he has a beautiful job here. Willy agrees: he is building something with this firm, but he cannot explain what until Linda reminds him about Singleman.	
Biff enters, followed by Happy, and Willy boasts about him to Ben, who walks out. Bernard enters. They are all off to watch the final match of the All-Scholastic Championship of the City of New York. Charley teases Willy, who does not appreciate his humour and, as Charley leaves, chuckling, Willy hurls abuse at him and challenges him to a fist fight.	

Commentary: **This sequence is prompted by Willy's contrasting memories and fears. Willy has confused the memory of Ben's one visit with the event that was the pinnacle of Willy's success as father of the captain of the triumphant football team. He would not have considered taking Biff away at this point, so the events cannot have coincided. Willy's concern that 'nothing's working out' shows that this is not a true memory — he is imagining his conversation with Ben. Willy is asking Ben's advice in the present, and he imagines Ben's responses.**

As usual, Willy imagines Ben to be in a hurry, chasing more business. Willy uses clichés to explain his dream to Ben, making Biff seem more destitute than he is by saying that he has not 'a penny to his name', and imagining Biff's potential for success to be immeasurable because 'the sky's the limit'.

Linda's dislike and fear of Ben is probably based on a memory. Willy remembers that Linda persuaded him not to move to Alaska, and she reminds Willy of his own stories about Singleman and 'old man Wagner's' promise of a partnership. It is unlikely that she believes in these stories, but she is a clever woman and knows that reminding Willy of them is the most successful way of keeping him in New York. The fact that she does not mention their hopes for Biff indicates that Willy's reminiscence is muddled.

As he approaches Charley's office, Willy remembers how Charley teased him about the Ebbets Field Game. For Willy this high school match became an event of tremendous significance because he thought it would decide Biff's future, but Charley makes jokes and asks Willy when he is going to grow up, wanting him to see things in perspective and not to set too

Context

Ebbets Field was a Major League Baseball park and professional football venue in the Flatbush section of Brooklyn, New York. The field was demolished in 1960 and replaced with apartment buildings.

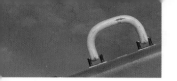

much store on a game. Willy fiercely resents Charley's banter and challenges Charley to a fist fight. Charley chuckles as he walks away, but Willy interprets this as mocking laughter. He is insulted and defensive. It is in this aggressive mood that he approaches Charley's office.

Act Two pp. 71–78

Psychic time	Social time
Willy is still abusing Charley and looking forward to the match.	Charley's secretary Jenny is '*distressed*'. Bernard greets Willy. Willy is impressed that Bernard's friends have a tennis court. He tries to make Biff's planned deal with Oliver sound impressive, but then breaks down and asks Bernard what the secret is.
	Bernard tells Willy that Biff's life ended after the Ebbets Field game. Biff planned to go to summer school to make up maths, then went to Boston to see Willy, came back a month later, burned his sneakers and had a fight with Bernard throughout which they both cried. Bernard realised then that Biff had given up on life and, although he took lots of correspondence courses, he never made the slightest mark. Willy reacts angrily, refusing to accept responsibility for Biff's failure.
	Charley enters and says goodbye to Bernard. Bernard is going to argue a case in front of the Supreme Court. Willy is impressed, particularly that Bernard did not mention it.
	Willy asks to borrow $110 but, when Charley offers him a job, acts as if insulted. Charley kindly asks how much he needs. Willy admits he has been fired, but still refuses a job. Willy is on the verge of tears and admits Charley is his only friend.

Commentary: **Jenny tells Bernard that Charley is upset every time Willy comes, reinforcing the audience's realisation that Charley's concern for Willy is genuine. Willy's crude joke is inappropriate and suggests that chatting up the secretaries is his technique as a salesman.**

Willy is '*almost shocked*' to see Bernard and approaches him '*guiltily*' but '*warmly*'. In all the imagined sequences he is dismissive of and insulting to Bernard, and this seems to trouble him. We realise Willy has exaggerated Bernard's 'anaemic' lack of masculinity because, after Biff's return from Boston, he and Bernard fought for at least half an hour, suggesting they were fairly evenly matched. Bernard's obvious quiet success prompts Willy to lie about Biff. Bernard's modesty leads him to answer Willy's question about his rich friends with a question about Willy's work, which is a delicate point as he has just been fired.

Willy praises Bernard, still trying to hope that his success 'looks very good for Biff', but then he breaks off: '*full of emotion*' and '*small and alone*', he asks Bernard 'What's the secret?' Willy

confides in Bernard and '*desperately*' asks what went wrong for Biff. At last we are aware of the reason why Willy keeps sliding back into the past — he is trying to understand what happened to Biff, but he has repressed the memory.

Bernard surprises Willy with a vital piece of information: before he went to Boston, Biff was ready to enrol in summer school. It was not failing maths that beat Biff but what happened in Boston. Biff burned the sneakers on which he had carefully printed 'University of Virginia' as a symbol of the abandonment of his academic hopes. Bernard says that Biff had 'given up on life', but he tried for several years to settle at a job in New York, so Bernard must mean that he had given up his ambitions.

When Bernard probes close to the fatal secret, by asking what happened in Boston, the shock of this revelation makes Willy look at him '*as at an intruder*'. Willy's feelings of guilt make him think that Bernard is blaming Biff's failure on him, whereas Willy has always blamed it on Mr Birnbaum. Until now, Willy has been able to say 'That son-of-a-bitch ruined his life.' Bernard diplomatically offers hope that Biff will change: 'If at first you don't succeed...', but suggests that Willy should walk away and let Biff sort out his own life. Willy's tragedy is that he cannot do this.

*Pause for **Thought***

Do you think the parent should still be blaming himself for the failings of a 34-year-old man?

When Willy learns about Bernard's success, he is '*shocked*' that Bernard has not mentioned the Supreme Court, '*pained*' that this proves that the values Charley instilled into his son were right, and yet still genuinely '*happy*' for Bernard. Charley casually gives Willy $50, but '*with difficulty*' Willy swallows his pride and asks for more to pay his insurance. It is not until later that we realise the significance of this small detail.

Once again, when Willy is unable to cope, he grows belligerent and puts up his fists to fight rather than admit he has been fired. When Charley does not take offence, however, and approaches him '*kindly*', Willy's aggression subsides and he confides in Charley. Charley offers him a job again and gets angry when Willy refuses, thinking that he does so out of jealousy, but Miller makes it clear that it is more complex than that. To accept a job with Charley would be to admit that he has had all the wrong dreams and the wrong values.

At last, Miller reveals that the reason Willy has been thinking of killing himself is that he feels that he is now 'worth more dead than alive'. He values everything in terms of money and, now that he can no longer sell his goods, he has only himself left to

❮ Top ten *quotation*

sell. Charley points out the obvious fact that nobody is worth anything dead but he realises that Willy is not listening. Willy is drifting into a dream world in which Biff is a success like Bernard, and Miller suggests that he is dreaming of how he can make this possible when he says, 'Wish me luck, Charley.' The only straw Willy has left to clutch at is that Biff might have good news to tell him after his meeting with Bill Oliver.

'*On the verge of tears*', Willy realises that Charley is his only friend and observes 'Isn't that a remarkable thing?' This is not remarkable to the audience but Miller gives Willy this phrase when he has a sudden realisation. He first uses it on p. 13 when he realises that he was confusing his cars as he drifted into a remembered sequence of driving the Chevrolet. Here it signifies surprise that all the people whom he values, whom he thought were his friends, have abandoned him, whereas Charley, a man whom he reviled and despised as less than a man, has always been there for him.

Act Two pp. 78–86

Psychic time	Social time
	'*Raucous music*' and '*a red glow*' introduce the restaurant. As Happy and Stanley talk, Miller makes it obvious that Happy is a regular customer and the waiter is going out of his way to please, expecting a big tip. Stanley sets a table on the forestage. Happy chats up a young woman, telling her he is a graduate from West Point and Biff is a famous footballer. She claims to be a cover girl but is evasive when Happy asks which magazine, suggesting she is also lying to impress. She goes to cancel her date and fetch a friend.
	Biff tells Happy that he waited in vain to see Bill Oliver, then impulsively stole a pen and ran. Happy tries to persuade him to tell Willy the deal is nearly clinched.
	Willy enters. Biff tries to tell the truth, but Happy chips in to tell Willy everything is fine. Willy gets angry at Biff's truths, tells them he was fired and is looking for good news to tell Linda. Biff and Happy between them get Willy confused, partly because Willy will not let Biff finish speaking.

Context

Officers-in-training at West Point Military Academy in New York are referred to as cadets. Ironically, the Cadet Honor Code states that 'a cadet will not lie, cheat, steal, or tolerate those who do'.

Commentary: **Happy is disappointed Miss Forsyth was so easy to seduce. He is looking for a woman 'with character, with resistance! Like Mom' (p. 19). While he enjoys sex with the women he casually picks up, he is looking for integrity in the woman he marries. Miller may be making a criticism of New York society here, but Happy is clearly attracted to women who dress '*lavishly*' like this one, wanting to be noticed by men. Stanley refers to her and Letta as 'chippies' which is a slang term for prostitutes.**

While Happy has been showing off, Biff has been diffident and, when the girl leaves, he is '*strangely unnerved*'. Biff's meeting with Bill Oliver has brought him face to face with the awareness that his whole life has been a 'ridiculous lie'. What has unnerved him is the realisation that he even believed the lies himself. He speaks '*with great tension and wonder*' because he has been forced to face the fact that he is a compulsive thief. '*Agonised*', he tells Happy that he does not know why he took the pen.

The lies still come easily to Happy, who wants his father to be happy, but Biff wants to get to the heart of the tension between him and his father and clear the air. Once again there is a hint of something between him and Willy: he knows Willy thinks he has acted out of spite. We do not yet know what it is, but this suggests that Biff is not blaming his father for his failure.

When his father enters, Biff goes '*to* WILLY *with guilt, as to an invalid*'. If Biff feels guilty, then this is an even clearer indication that he does not blame his father. With dramatic irony the audience now knows that Willy is even more fragile, having lost his job, and that he has learned that Biff gave up on life after his visit to Boston, so he has more reason to blame himself.

Miller indicates how much of a strain this confession is on Biff because '*his breath keeps breaking the rhythm of his voice*'. Nevertheless, he speaks '*with determination*', forcing Willy to listen, but his father gets angry — he is desperate for some good news to give Linda, so it is suddenly more difficult to tell him the truth.

Because Willy has not achieved the spectacular success he dreams of, he has pinned all his hopes on Biff. Biff feels under great pressure to live up to his father's expectations but he believes that he will never be able to do it because he is 'not the man somebody lends that kind of money to'. Biff is learning to know himself. Happy, however, gives Willy what he wants to hear, and between them they manoeuvre Biff into lying. This makes him angry, and he makes Willy angry, so once again they cannot speak to each other. By this point, Miller has dropped enough hints for the audience to understand the nature of the catastrophe.

Taking it
Further

Watch the restaurant scene from the television production with Warren Mitchell. Go to www.youtube.com and search for 'Death of a Salesman Warren Mitchell'.

Act Two pp. 86–97

Psychic time	Social time
Willy imagines the scene when Bernard told Linda that Biff failed maths and went to Boston. Clearly this is not a memory, as Willy was in Boston.	Biff and Happy are confused by what Willy is saying. He is speaking '*wildly*' and '*furiously*', telling Biff that, if he had not flunked maths, he would have been set by now. Biff struggles to tell his father the truth, but the light fades on the restaurant and, although Biff continues talking, neither Willy nor the audience can hear what he says.
Willy is now immersed in the imagined past when Biff made the fateful decision to go to Boston. Willy remembers hearing the operator's voice ringing him in his hotel room in Boston. Willy tries to silence the operator.	
	As Willy is gradually recalled to the present, Biff has finished his story and is holding up the stolen pen. As Willy realises that Biff stole it, the past intrudes again.
Willy is paged at the hotel.	
Willy hears the operator's voice and shouts that he is not in his room.	Willy has no awareness that he is in a restaurant. Biff, '*frightened*' and '*horrified*' tries to calm Willy down. Biff gets down on one knee before Willy, who tells him he is no good for anything. Biff '*desperately*' lies about having an appointment with Oliver. He is frightened at what is happening to Willy and is trying to bring Willy back to sanity. On this optimistic note, Willy returns to the present and tells Biff to say that the pen was an oversight. '*Agonised*' Biff tries not to raise his hopes and, despairing once again, Willy lapses into the past.
Willy attempts '*to stand, as though to rush and silence the operator*'.	
Willy hears the page's voice.	
	Willy is convinced that Biff is refusing to go to the fictional appointment out of spite, and Biff gets angry, wanting Willy to realise how much it cost him to swallow his pride and go back to Oliver. He went only because he loves his father, and he is '*now angry at* WILLY *for not crediting his sympathy*'.
The woman laughs.	
	Willy strikes Biff, who makes one final attempt to make his father see reason and then ignores him. Happy separates them. The girls enter and sit down.
The woman laughs again.	
	Biff tells them he has been before a jury, as if he's joking.
There is someone at the door. We hear the woman laugh and try to wake Willy up. She urges Willy to open the door. She tries to get Willy out of bed.	Willy is '*befuddled*'. Biff is urging him to sit with them and drink, but at the same time Willy hears the woman '*urgently*' telling him to open the door. He is about to sit but goes out, asking for the washroom.

The woman insists he get up.

Resentful of the presence of the girls in this painfully private family confrontation, Biff delivers a eulogy of his father. In his distress and desperation, Biff unfairly rounds on Happy and puts the rolled up hose on the table. He accuses Happy of not doing anything for Willy, of not caring and of not realising that Willy is planning to kill himself. Happy is flabbergasted at the unjust attack. Then, '*ready to weep*', Biff hurries out, begging Happy to help Willy and to help him.

Happy follows Biff with the two women and denies his father. Stanley, indignant, follows them, calling to Happy, 'Mr Loman! Mr Loman!'

The woman laughs and Willy begs her not to open the door.

In Willy's mind, Stanley's call becomes the hotel page calling him from outside the door. The woman enters in a black slip. Willy follows, buttoning his shirt. Willy does not want to answer the door and, as the knocking continues, his terror rises. Reluctantly, he pushes her into the bathroom, telling her that there's a law against adultery in Massachusetts. He opens the door to Biff.

Biff has failed maths. He is so proud of his father that he is convinced that Willy would be able to persuade Mr Birnbaum to give him the extra points. Biff says the reason the teacher hates him is because he imitated his lisp in class, and gives a demonstration. Willy laughs and the woman joins in. Willy tries to cover up the situation but the woman laughs again.

She enters and Willy tries to push her out, but she demands the two boxes of stockings he promised her. Biff collapses on his suitcase. Willy tries to give some harmless explanation but Biff will not listen. Willy kneels beside him and tries to talk him round. Biff ignores Willy's orders. He weeps silently but his sobs break from him as he accuses Willy of giving the woman Linda's stockings, and rushes out. His faith in his father is shattered, and he no longer believes his teacher would listen to Willy, whom he sees as a 'phony little fake'. Willy is still on his knees.

Stanley enters and helps Willy up. Willy worries about his appearance and presses money on Stanley, who secretly gives it back. Willy asks for directions to a seed store.

Commentary: **Biff does not understand why Willy is talking about him failing maths, and this indicates that he does not link his lack of success with his failure to graduate. It seems unlikely that Willy would have tried to avoid responding to the call in the hotel at the time, but in his imagination he is trying to prevent the disaster that revealed his infidelity to Biff. His memory of the incident is distorted by his subsequent**

Context

Massachusetts is one of five states that, at least on paper, still considers adultery a felony. Many more states consider it to be a misdemeanour.

knowledge of the identity of the visitor and, with hindsight, he desperately tries to prevent the catastrophe from occurring.

In a betrayal reminiscent of Peter's denial of Christ, Happy says that Willy is not his father, 'just a guy'. Happy has seen his father's slow deterioration, was driving with him the previous week, and he paid for their holiday in Florida. He knows that most of the time Willy is talking to Biff and that his problems seem to be rooted in the fact that Biff is not settled. Happy was the one who went down to help his father (p. 32). He has had time to get used to Willy's condition and to learn that there is very little he can do to help, except to try to keep Willy happy. Biff has not been home for a year, and so Willy's mental disintegration is a shock to him.

The woman's laugh has haunted Willy since p. 29 and has clearly been associated with a bad memory. In this scene we find out why. It was her laugh that revealed her presence to Biff. Biff's explanation for his appearance in Boston, 'I let you down', reinforces our impression that Biff was attempting to fulfil his father's ambition, not his own. Biff assumes that the maths teacher is being spiteful in revenge for Biff's cruel mockery, rather than accepting that Mr Birnbaum does not think him worthy of graduation because he misses lessons, does no work, and relies on Bernard to give him the answers.

Because Miller has given hints of the revelation about the woman and the audience has already guessed the secret at the heart of the play, this scene is not the climax. We are still waiting for that. Miller has carefully arranged it so that Willy is on his knees, having been abandoned for the third time in his life, and then his theme tune is played.

Willy gives Stanley a dollar, possibly in an attempt to prove to himself that he has something to give to someone. Young Stanley's kindness to Willy contrasts markedly with his sons' behaviour, but Willy's comment 'I don't need it any more' suggests that this is where he decides to end it all. He hurries off to buy some seeds, symbolic of a future. Ominously, he wants to leave something behind him.

*Pause for **Thought***

What difference might it have made to the plot if Willy had heard how Biff describes him to the girls?

Task 2

Miller makes it clear that finding Willy with a woman was a shattering experience for Biff and one which prompted his decision to abandon his plans to go to university. What evidence can you find that this was not the only reason that he has not made a success of his life?

Task 3

Why do you think Miller introduces Willy's theme music at the point when he realises that his sons have abandoned him?

Act Two pp. 97–109

Psychic time	Social time
	Biff and Happy return to the house. Linda is off-stage but she '*rises ominously and quietly*', advancing on Happy who backs away '*afraid*'. Happy attempts a couple of light-hearted questions, but Linda is silent and moves towards him '*implacably*' as he continues backing away from her. The audience sees only Happy's reaction and we watch fascinated as she moves into full view in the doorway. She ignores Happy's nervous chatter and magnificently knocks the proffered roses to the floor at Biff's feet.
	'*She stares at* Biff, *silent*', ignores Happy, cutting across his chatter to '*violently*' accuse Biff. She defends Willy like a tigress defending her young, ordering them out and refusing to let Biff near Willy. She stops herself from picking up the flowers. She continues in this commanding vein until Willy's presence in the garden is revealed by humming, then she suddenly pleads with Biff to leave Willy alone.
	Happy wants to avoid this confrontation, but Biff distances himself from Happy '*with a flare of disgust*'. Biff looks for Willy. As he '*slowly moves over and gets down on his knees*' to pick up the flowers, the audience realises the depth of his penitence. He cannot look at his mother and '*violently*' tells Happy to shut up when he starts lying. Still kneeling, Biff speaks with '*self-loathing*', admitting his neglect of Willy and agreeing with her contempt. He gets up, throws the roses in a waste basket and accuses himself of being 'the scum of the earth'. '*With absolute assurance, determination*' he asserts that he is going to have 'an abrupt conversation' with Willy.
Ben appears and Willy asks his advice about his plan. He feels he must add up to something for Linda because she has suffered. At this point, the proposition is to kill himself so Linda can collect the life insurance.	As Biff and Linda watch, Willy plants seeds.
Gradually, he forgets Linda and reveals that, because he feels guilty and thinks Biff is vindictive towards him, he wants to show Biff that he is popular and valued. He imagines a funeral like that of Singleman, attended by buyers and salesmen from the seven states where he has worked.	
Willy imagines the responses Ben might make and reacts to them. When Ben agrees that $20,000 is a significant sum (in 1948 it would have been equivalent to around $200,000 today), Willy is '*now assured, with rising power*'. When Ben suggests that Biff will call him a 'coward' and 'a damned fool', he is '*suddenly fearful*', '*broken and desperate*'. As Ben voices Willy's fear that Biff will hate him, he remembers the wonderful relationship he had with his sons before the fateful day in Boston. As always, Willy imagines Ben to be in a hurry, and Ben '*drifts off*', unnoticed.	

Biff's presence brings Willy back to consciousness of the present. Biff says goodbye. Willy, who still believes what he was told in the restaurant, cannot understand why Biff refuses to go to the appointment with Oliver. Biff tries to make it up with Willy without apportioning blame. He tries to take Willy indoors to show Linda they are pals once more. Willy's guilt after the memory of the woman makes him freeze, '*immobile*'. '*Highly nervous*', he refuses to see her.

Biff does not understand. He reassures Willy that his failure is his own fault, not his father's. Surprisingly, Linda agrees that Biff should go and not even write any more, because it upsets Willy whenever he does. Willy is silent throughout this exchange but, when Biff holds out his hand to say goodbye and Linda urges him to take it, Willy reveals he still believes Biff is refusing to go to the appointment to spite him. Willy is '*seething with hurt*' and refuses to listen to Biff's confession. Biff sadly turns to go and Willy curses him violently, still believing Biff cut down his life to spite Willy because of seeing him with the woman. Willy's guilty feelings show in his refusal to take the blame. Willy sinks into a chair, accusing Biff of '*trying to put a knife in me*'.

Goaded beyond patience, Biff confronts Willy with the rubber tubing. Willy is '*caged, wanting to escape*', but Biff is relentless. Worried, Happy tries to intervene, but Biff turns on him, telling the truth about Happy's 'success' and about his own spell in prison. Linda sobs, but Biff continues to tell the stark truth, including a list of the things he loves.

In Oliver's office he had suddenly realised that everything he wants is waiting for him, the minute he accepts who he is. Willy, '*with hatred, threateningly*', refuses to let go of his dream that Biff will be a big success. The only way Willy can explain Biff's abandonment of the dream is to say that he is acting out of spite.

'*In his fury,* Biff *seems on the verge of attacking his father*', but Happy blocks him. When Biff breaks from Happy, 'Willy*, in fright, starts up the stairs*' and, '*at the peak of his fury*', Biff grabs him and '*breaks down, sobbing, holding on to* Willy*, who dumbly fumbles for* Biff*'s face*'.

'*Astonished*' and '*elevated*' by the realisation that Biff cares about him, Willy's voice is '*choking with his love, and now cries out its promise...That boy is going to be magnificent.*' He has not heard or accepted what Biff has been telling him, and he still believes that all Biff needs to be a success is the money to get started.

Ben comes in and tells Willy that, with $20,000 behind him, Biff will be a success.

Linda has not heard Ben's words, but she '*senses the racing of* [Willy's] *mind*' and '*fearfully, carefully*' tries to calm Willy down and get him to bed.

In accents of dread, BEN's *'idyllic music starts up.'* Willy imagines Ben encouraging him, comparing the act of killing himself for money to going into the dark jungle for diamonds. Just as it takes 'a great kind of man to crack the jungle', so Willy hopes that he will be a great man if he can generate the insurance money for Biff. This is the only way he can emulate his successful brother.

Willy almost dances over to Ben, imagining that, when the cheque arrives in the post, Biff will be 'ahead of Bernard again' — he still has that urge to compete. Ben moves off to catch a boat and Willy speaks *'elegiacally'* of Biff at his peak, preparing for the big match.

Willy reassures Linda, promising to follow her to bed. When Linda speaks of Biff's staying away as 'the only way', Willy picks up her words, but he is thinking of killing himself as 'the best thing'. We can see Linda in the bedroom as we watch and listen to Willy. Willy is jubilant because Biff loves him and thinks Biff will 'worship' him for the opportunity he is about to create. Twice Willy declares it to be 'remarkable' that Biff likes him.

Suddenly Willy loses his imagined contact with Ben and utters *'a gasp of fear'*, whirling about as if to shush Linda, who calls him. *'He turns around as if to find his way; sounds, faces, voices seem to be swarming in upon him and he flicks at them, crying* 'Sh! Sh!' *Suddenly music, faint and high, stops him. It rises in intensity, almost to an unbearable scream. He goes up and down on his toes, and rushes off around the house.'* Linda and Biff call him.

The rest of the story is told in music and mime as, after *'the music crashes down in a frenzy of sound'*, signifying the car crash, it becomes *'the soft pulsation of a single 'cello string.'* Willy's family and his neighbours *'slowly'* and *'gravely'* make their preparations and gather at the front of the stage, staring down at the grave.

Commentary: **Ironically, immediately after Willy's repressed memory of his infidelity and Biff's disillusionment, we see evidence of Linda's intense loyalty to him as she pours scorn on their two sons. Willy thinks that killing himself would make him 'add up to something', which is poignantly ironic because he does add up to something: he is a much-loved husband and father, and he has succeeded in paying off the house that he has significantly improved. He does not value these achievements, however, thinking that he would be a success only if he had made a great deal of money. His sense of self-worth is so low that, as he told Charley, he thinks he is worth 'more dead than alive'. Clearly his discussions with Ben are not a memory. He has conjured up Ben in his imagination because he cannot discuss his plan with anyone else.**

❰ Top ten *quotation*

Taking it
Further ➤
∙∙∙∙∙∙∙∙∙∙∙∙∙∙∙∙∙∙∙∙∙∙∙∙
Watch Iain Glen confront Warren Mitchell with the truth. Go to www.youtube. com and search for 'Death of a Salesman scene Warren Mitchell'.
∙∙∙∙∙∙∙∙∙∙∙∙∙∙∙∙∙∙∙∙∙∙∙∙

*Pause for **Thought***

Do you agree that, once Biff's love for his father is revealed, there could have been a happy ending?

The whole play has been leading up to the fight between Biff and Willy, when all the resentment is dissipated, and Biff's love for his father is finally revealed. This is the peak of emotional intensity, the climax of the play when all the tension is released. At this point, the play could still have a happy ending, but Willy refuses to let go of his dream, being obsessed with the notion that wealth is necessary for success. This makes Willy's death inevitable.

Requiem

Psychic time	Social time
	Linda is still sitting on her heels, staring at the grave. It seems she believed Willy's stories of his popularity, since she is surprised that nobody has come to the funeral, wondering whether they blame him for committing suicide. She does not understand why Willy should take his own life when he has achieved so much.
	Only Charley understands Willy and why he could not let go of his dream, and he speaks eloquently in Willy's defence.
	Happy is angry, declaring 'We would've helped him', and aggressive towards Biff, who realises that Willy's dreams were 'All, all, wrong'. Happy intends to fight for Willy's dream in New York.
	Biff has happy memories and no longer blames Willy, realising that Willy did not know who he was. He looks hopelessly at Happy, realising that he is still deluded. Linda remains sitting at the graveside asking Willy's forgiveness because she cannot cry. As she begins to sob, Biff '*lifts her to her feet and moves out up right with her in his arms*'.

Commentary: **Willy thinks that Biff will worship him for providing the insurance money. He imagines a 'massive' funeral and that 'that boy will be thunderstruck, Ben, because he never realised — I am known!...he'll see it with his eyes once and for all.' However, Miller offers the final proof that Willy had all the wrong dreams because nobody comes to the funeral, not even his boss. Miller has ironically called the final scene 'Requiem', which refers to the Catholic mass calling for the eternal rest of the dead. However, the five mourners are not praying. They do not look forward to a glorious afterlife but lament a meaningless death.**

All the characters who previously took part in Willy's 'private conversations' are now supposedly free, but they will never be free of him. Linda, who has known what he was planning all along, now says that she does not

understand why he was not satisfied with what he had. She repeats that 'we're free', but there is 'nobody home'. Happy is still living with Willy's dream and is determined to achieve it for his father. Biff now has a firmer grasp on reality, and he says that he knows who he is, but does that mean he will be able to stop stealing and take on his responsibilities as a member of a family?

Task **4**

As a class, set up an inquest into Willy's death. You will need a lawyer and a coroner, a representative of the insurance company, a psychologist and characters from the play as witnesses. If it is proven that Willy committed suicide, the insurance company will not pay out.

Themes

The American Dream

Context

The Founding Fathers are the political leaders who signed the Declaration of Independence in 1776.

Taking it
Further

Read the full text of the Declaration of Independence at www. ushistory.org/declaration/ document/

Although this term was not coined until the twentieth century, the concept has its roots in the American Declaration of Independence in 1776. The Founding Fathers of America set out their vision in the justification for breaking away from British rule: 'We hold these Truths to be self-evident that all men are created equal, that they are endowed, by their Creator, with certain unalienable Rights, that among these are Life, Liberty and the Pursuit of Happiness.' Immigrants to America were escaping from oppressive government, from conflict, from resistance to progress, from poverty, and they saw America as a blank slate upon which they could create their vision of a perfect state completely free from the inequalities of life in the Old World.

Originally the Founding Fathers had a dream that every man would have the same opportunity to earn enough money to have a stake in society and raise a family. They wanted to create a land of opportunity where success did not depend on birth or privilege but on hard work and courage. To the Founding Fathers, wealth meant sufficient riches to provide 'wellness'. This is the version of the dream to which Linda adheres. To her, Willy is doing 'wonderful'; it is an 'accomplishment' to weather a 25-year mortgage. Having started with nothing, now, at the age of 63, Willy owns a house in an affluent neighbourhood where 'The street is lined with cars' (p. 12). He also has a car, a refrigerator, a vacuum cleaner and a telephone, modern conveniences that were not universally owned in 1948. He has brought up two children who love him, and his wife adores him. By the original standards of the American Dream, Willy has achieved it.

In the middle of the nineteenth century, there was high unemployment in the cities of the Eastern Seaboard, and the fertile farmland of the West was seen as an ideal place for people willing to work hard for the opportunity to succeed. Many were encouraged to venture into undiscovered territory and travel west. Willy's father followed these pioneers in the hope of fulfilling his dreams in the great outdoors. He took his family in a wagon, selling flutes that he had made himself, and the flute music that accompanies Willy's happy memories suggests that this was an idyllic time for the young child. However, the whole country had been explored and settled by that time, and there were fewer opportunities. In 1889, his father abandoned his wife and children to go to Alaska, probably to join the gold rush, following a corrupted version of the Dream, which promised to make a man rich quickly.

Willy sees Ben as the embodiment of the American Dream: 'success incarnate' (p. 32). Willy remembers that he had an opportunity when Ben invited him to go to Alaska. This choice puts in stark contrast the two versions of the Dream. The Founding Fathers envisaged a new world where every man has the opportunity to achieve a stake in society. Ben offered Willy the debased version that every man has the right to walk into the jungle and come out rich. Willy chose the first and stayed in New York, but he continues to dream of the second.

The original version of the American Dream belonged to a rural America, but with the Industrial Revolution people flocked to the towns. The image of America changed from that of a log cabin to a thrusting skyscraper, and the word 'wealth' came to suggest abundant riches. The modern version of the Dream sets the independent pioneer in the world of business, where he is once again able to get to the top relying only on his talents and hard work. Anyone can become successful; anyone can accumulate riches. This is the version of the Dream Willy believes in and he is scathing about Biff's decision to go west where all he can do is 'Be a carpenter, a cowboy, enjoy [him]self!' (p. 48).

Ben is an example of how the Dream can be used to excuse ruthless determination. Willy views Ben as another adventurous father figure who achieved the Dream when he walked into the jungle at 17 and walked out again at 21, rich. Like his father, however, Ben abandoned his responsibilities, caring so little about his mother that he did not even know that she had died. It seems that Ben did not become rich as a result of hard work but through 'walking' into the jungle. Four years in a diamond mine, however, does not sound as easy as he implies.

Ben's methods are illustrated when he teaches Biff, 'Never fight fair with a stranger' (p. 38) and shows approval of Biff's theft of building materials under the eyes of the watchman. Miller juxtaposes the drawbacks of their versions of the American Dream as Willy imagines Ben advising him to get out of cities with their 'talk and time payments and courts of law' and to 'screw on' his fists and 'fight for a fortune' in Alaska (p. 66).

By contrast, in Charley, Miller provides us with an example of someone who has achieved the American Dream by following the example of the Founding Fathers. He started modestly and has built up a successful

Context

Christopher Bigsby quotes Miller as saying that: 'America is hope, even when it doesn't work…America is promises…I don't think America ever got over the Depression.'

Context

Miller wrote that 'I was ironically stating all the things that they always state seriously. A man can get anywhere in this country on the basis of being liked. Now this is serious advice, and the audience is sitting out there almost about to smile [in disbelief], but the tears are coming out of their eyes because they know that that is what they believe' (*The Theater Essays of Arthur Miller*, 1996).

business. His son has worked hard and is about to argue a case in front of the Supreme Court. Unlike Happy's merchandise manager, who built a 'terrific estate' on Long Island but sold it because he 'can't enjoy it once it's finished' (p. 17), Charley still lives in the modest house next to Willy where Bernard grew up. Charley has his feet on the ground and has not become contaminated by the new version of the Dream. He is contented, compassionate and understanding.

Willy is a hard-working salesman, 'at it ten, twelve hours a day', but he is not satisfied with his achievements. The version of the dream on which he has based his life is that exemplified by Dave Singleman who, at the age of 84, could sell from his hotel room by just lifting the phone, and whose funeral was attended by hundreds of salesmen and buyers. For Willy, the love of his family is not enough: he needs to be 'well-liked' and feels a failure because he is not. Willy's identity is rooted in his job and he imagines working until he dies on the job as Singleman did. However, if this legendary salesman was still travelling at 84, surely he was not as successful as Willy seems to think.

Willy has taught his sons that studying is not important, because, if you are popular, someone else will give you the answers. According to Willy, honesty is not important, because, if you are well-liked, the coach will praise your initiative when you steal a ball. It is more important to be a 'fearless character', like Ben. For Biff, the American Dream has become a nightmare, demonstrated by the way the Wild West, symbolic of freedom and opportunity, became the place where he was thrown into jail. Biff would be happy being a 'bum', working on the land under the sky with 'time to sit and smoke' (p. 105), if it were not for his father's expectation that he should be a spectacular success. The play ends as it began with flute music evoking this rural idyll, while the 'hard towers of the apartment buildings' symbolise the materialism that has corrupted the Dream in the modern world. Nothing has changed.

The problem seems to lie in the wording of the Declaration. If 'happiness' is defined as a 'right' and regarded as an entitlement like 'life' and 'liberty', then the Declaration of Independence can be interpreted as promising wealth to all and justifying the actions of those who pursue success at any cost, like Ben. Anyone who is not ruthless and determined enough to achieve it is made to feel a failure, like Willy. Charley demonstrates that the dream can be achieved by just getting on with your life, keeping the law, working hard and letting your children develop naturally. 'Happiness' does not lie in the pursuit of wealth; as Charley says, 'My salvation is that I never took any interest in anything' (p. 75).

Taking it Further

Other archetypal 'American Dream' texts you might enjoy comparing with *Salesman* include F. Scott Fitzgerald's *The Great Gatsby*, John Steinbeck's *Of Mice and Men* and Tennessee Williams's *A Streetcar Named Desire* and *Cat on a Hot Tin Roof*.

Context

In 1964, Miller said, 'The job is to ask questions — it always was — and to ask them as inexorably as I can. And to face the absence of precise answers with a certain humility' (*National Observer*).

Reality and illusion

To dramatise the blurring of the distinction between illusion and reality in Willy's mind, Miller also blurs the distinction in the set and the structure of the play. The set enables the illusion and reality to be enacted simultaneously, and the play is so structured that it is not always clear what the reality is. Willy dreams of success that it is not possible for him to achieve, and he constantly exaggerates in order to create the illusion for those around him that he is successful. The Requiem makes clear that, if Willy had been true to himself, he would never have become a salesman nor lived in the city.

Biff says 'he never knew who he was' (p. 111). When Miller was asked what Willy was selling, he answered 'Himself.' All his life he has been selling himself so that people will buy his products simply because they like him. The result is that he is unable to separate himself as a husband and father from his conception of himself as a salesman. In Howard's office, he tries so hard to sell himself to Howard that he loses his job.

Willy is also totally unrealistic about what Biff might be able to achieve, and he has passed this inability to face the truth on to his sons. Happy exaggerates his position in the company and seems to sincerely believe that he is honest, in spite of accepting bribes and seducing other men's fiancées. Biff has distorted memories of the past, saying of Bill Oliver: 'He did like me. Always liked me' (p. 51). Later, however, he is forced to admit that he was just a shipping clerk, and Oliver does not even recognise him. Biff realises only then that he has been lying to himself for years about the position he held in the company. By the end of the day, Biff realises that it is this inability to distinguish between reality and illusion that has destroyed the family, and he is determined to make Willy face the truth.

Alienation

Willy Loman's feelings of alienation and loneliness are the direct psychological results of his interaction with society. Although he cannot define his feelings as such, they are revealed in his constant bragging and attempted compensations. He does not feel that he is truly a part of society. He tells Linda, 'people don't seem to take to me' and 'they seem to laugh at me' (p. 28). Willy desperately wants to command respect, like Charley. Although usually he pretends that he has a valued place in society, he does at times admit his feelings to his wife.

Task 5

What evidence are we given to help us distinguish between illusion and reality? For instance:

- Did Ben really give Willy a diamond fob watch?
- Did Biff really possess great potential?
- Was Willy really vital in New England?

Context

Miller wrote of the first film: 'March was directed to play Willy as a psycho, all but completely out of control with next to no grip on reality... the misconception melted the tension between a man and his society, drawing the teeth of the play's social contemporaneity, obliterating its very context. If he was nuts, he could hardly stand as a comment on anything' (*Timebends*).

Taking it
Further

Look at the original poster designed by Joseph Hirsch and consider how he has suggested Willy's alienation from society: http://tinyurl.com/32v728g/

Context

Raymond Williams writes: 'it is…the image of the Salesman that predominates. The social figure sums up the theme of alienation, for this is a man who from selling things has passed to selling himself, and has become…a commodity which…will at a certain point be economically discarded.' (*Drama from Ibsen to Brecht*, 1964).

Underneath his public persona, Willy knows that he is a failure. He can no longer provide for his family and he has let them down. Not only has he betrayed Linda with 'the Woman', but he has failed in his intention to leave a business for the boys. This is why he feels alienated. Willy talks to himself to try to understand what went wrong and he seeks advice from his dead brother, Ben, on how to help his sons become successful. Willy also confides in Bernard, trying to understand why Biff has made nothing of his life: 'I got nobody to talk to. Bernard, Bernard, was it my fault? Y'see? It keeps going around in my mind, maybe I did something to him' (p. 73). However, when Bernard is candid with him, Willy is angry, refusing to accept the blame. His feelings of guilt isolate him to a degree where he cannot talk to anyone but himself.

Biff also feels alienated from American society, and it is Willy who sums this up when he laments uncomprehendingly: 'In the greatest country in the world, a young man with such — personal attractiveness, gets lost' (p. 11). It seems that it was not only the knowledge of his father's infidelity that alienated Biff from society. After that, he spent several years trying to build himself up in the city, but he hated the 'measly manner of existence' (p. 16). He loves the outdoor life but is expected to settle down, get married and build a future in the city.

The family

Context

In an interview with Matthew C. Roudané in 1987, Miller said of *Death of a Salesman*, '…it involves some of the most rudimentary elements in the civilizing process: family cohesion, death and dying, parricide, rebirth, and so on…People feel these themes no matter where they are.'

In the world of *Death of a Salesman*, the family is seen as the basis of society. Even the minor characters are presented in terms of family. Charley's son Bernard is married with two children; Howard's family is brought on stage through the device of the tape recorder; even Ben is married and has seven sons. Stanley declares 'a family business… that's the best' (p. 79). The fact that neither Biff nor Happy is married compounds their sense of failure, and Happy's empty promise that he is getting married is purely an attention-seeking device.

There is no doubt of Willy's love for his family. He perceives the root of the family's problems to be his betrayal of Linda, and it is out of loyalty to his family that he sacrifices himself.

However, his own father walked out before Willy was four years old. All he knows about his legendary father is that he was supposedly a man of extraordinary talents: he was a pioneer, an inventor, a musician, a craftsman and a salesman who 'made more in a week than a man like you could make in a lifetime' (p. 38). This is a daunting role model to live up to. Willy tries hard to be a good father. He is patriotic, calling the USA 'the greatest country in the world' (p. 11). He passes on to the boys what he learns about its history and tries to teach them values like those of Benjamin Franklin. He tells them: 'You want to watch your schooling first' and 'Never leave a job till you're finished' (pp. 21, 22). Happy has been taught to respect girls, so, when he sleeps with them, he thinks they are 'ruined'. He has been taught the importance of honesty and hates himself when he takes bribes.

The Loman family in the 2005 London production of the play, with Brian Dennehy as Willy and Clare Higgins as Linda

Willy lacks confidence in the role of father, seeking Ben's approval for his efforts, and, under what he believes to be Ben's influence, he brings his sons up to be 'fearless characters', 'rugged, well-liked, all-around' with the spirit 'to walk into a jungle' or steal sand from a building site (pp. 39, 38, 41). In the Loman family, the sense of order created by the family unit is threatened because it is based on illusions and delusions. Realising that he will never achieve the kind of magnificent success he dreams of, Willy, as so many parents do, has transferred his dreams and ambitions on to his sons, particularly Biff, his firstborn.

He sees Biff as 'Adonis', 'a young god', 'Hercules' and 'magnificent', and this is why he cannot accept that he and Biff are 'a dime a dozen'. To Willy, the high school football match was some kind of ancient ritual in which the young god proved his worth in front of the representatives of three colleges and the buyers Willy wanted to impress. In present time, Willy clings to the dream that Biff will still prove his 'magnificence'. Willy's distorted understanding of the role of a father reaches a tragic climax when he thinks that Biff will 'worship' him for killing himself for the insurance money. He cannot accept that to love your family is enough.

Context

Miller wrote that the Loman home was based on that of his uncle, travelling salesman Manny Newman. Miller described it as one in which you 'dared not lose hope, and I would later think of it as a perfection of America for that reason…It was a house trembling with resolution and shouts of victories that had not yet taken place but surely would tomorrow' (*Timebends*).

Taking it Further ▶

Tennessee Williams's *Cat on a Hot Tin Roof* features a very similar family structure to that of the Lomans in *Salesman*: a dominant father, an undervalued mother, an idolised and favoured son and a less valued son. A study of the ways in which Miller and Williams present these families would make an excellent comparative coursework assignment.

Context

The production that Miller directed in Beijing in 1983 focused on Willy's ambitions for his sons and the father–son relationship. China has a long tradition of children honouring their parents but it had few salesmen then, as it was just beginning to emerge as a capitalist country.

Biff does not have the same feelings about the match and does not even take his athletic trophy when he leaves home. In spite of his disillusionment about his father, Biff still loves him and wants to please him, but the weight of Willy's expectations destroys Biff because he cannot be contented living the life he loves. Having absorbed his father's values, Biff tells Happy, 'I've always made a point of not wasting my life, and every time I come back here I know that all I've done is to waste my life' (p. 17).

Willy and his sons would all be happier in a rural environment but Willy's false dream keeps him in the city where the family does not belong. Willy is distracted by the scenery as he drives. He wishes he had gone to Alaska and reminisces nostalgically about the past when the house was surrounded by trees and flowers. He dreams of owning 'a little place out in the country' (p. 56). He feels boxed in by 'bricks and windows' and the stink from the apartment houses, and these claustrophobic feelings seem to make him aggressive, like a caged animal, and force him to live in his mind to escape. Happy dreams of owning a ranch with Biff, and he knows he could 'outbox, outrun, and outlift anybody in that store' (p. 18), but he is trapped by the dream of becoming merchandise manager and having the waves of employees part in front of him. Only Biff has escaped from the city he hates, but he feels guilty about it.

Miller focuses particularly on the relationship between father and son. He wrote in his Introduction: 'In writing of the father–son relationship and of the son's search for his relatedness there was a fullness of feeling I had never known before. The crux of *All My Sons* was formed; and the roots of *Death of a Salesman* were sprouted.' Linda tells Biff and Happy that Willy was, 'The man who never worked a day but for your benefit', and that he loved his sons 'better than his life' (p. 45). For Biff, Willy has been an idealised role model whom he rejects when he realises his idol is flawed. For Willy, Biff is still the golden boy who will realise his father's dreams, and any failure in Biff he interprets as spite against himself. Nevertheless, both father and son love and need each other. It is in exploring this complex relationship that Miller creates dramatic tensions that come to no conclusion but exert such power over the audience.

Characters

Willy Loman

In *Salesman in Beijing*, Miller wrote that Willy 'is the walking believer, the bearer of a flame whose going-out would leave us flat'. However, Willy is no conventional hero. He has a 'mercurial nature' and a 'temper'. He hit another salesman in the face when he overheard him 'say something about — walrus' (p. 29), he twice challenges Charley to a fist-fight, and he 'strikes Biff' in the restaurant. He often treats his family and friends with contempt, exercising '*little cruelties*' (p. 8). He is not very clever or well educated and lays himself open to ridicule by thinking he knows more than he does, such as when he lectures Charley about vitamins. He exaggerates, fabricates and boasts; he cannot understand why Bernard did not tell him that he was going to be arguing a case at the Supreme Court. He is a flawed individual, recognisable and familiar to most of Miller's audience.

In his autobiography, *Timebends*, Miller wrote that he based Willy Loman largely on his uncle, Manny Newman, who was a travelling salesman. He started planning the play after a chance meeting with his uncle: 'I could see his grim hotel behind him, the long trip up from New York in his little car, the hopeless hope of the day's business. Without so much as acknowledging my greeting, he said, "Buddy is doing very well".' According to Miller, his uncle was 'a competitor at all times, in all things, and at every moment'. His uncle saw 'my brother and I running neck and neck with his two sons in some horse race that never stopped in his mind'. In *Timebends*, Miller wrote that his uncle

> **...was so absurd, so completely isolated from the ordinary laws of gravity, so elaborate in his fantastic inventions, and...so lyrically in love with fame and fortune and their inevitable descent on his family, that he possessed my imagination until I knew more or less precisely how he would react to any sign or word or idea...but always underneath was the river of his sadness.**

Willy's tragedy is that, as Biff recognises after Willy's death, 'He had the wrong dreams' (p. 110). Although he comes from a pioneering family, Willy has pinned his 'massive dreams' on financial success in the world of business. He is convinced that popularity and personal attractiveness

Context

Miller wrote: 'In later years I found it discouraging to observe the confidence with which some commentators... smirked at the heavy-handed symbolism of 'Low-man'. What the name really meant to me was a terror-stricken man calling into the void for help that will never come' (*Timebends*).

Context

In 1984, Miller wrote: 'Willy is...ridiculous sometimes...He tells the most transparent lies, exaggerates mercilessly...But... his impulses are not foolish at all. He cannot bear reality, and, since he can't...change it, he keeps changing his ideas of it' (*Salesman in Beijing*).

provide the key to this success and that he must demonstrate his success by buying modern appliances. Being unable to purchase them outright, Willy has bought them on an instalment plan so they are worn out before he has paid for them.

He tells Howard that, after he met Dave Singleman, he 'realised that selling was the greatest career a man could want' (p. 63). However, although he is extremely hard-working and has managed to provide for his wife and family until shortly before the play opens, he has never been good at it. His personality is wrong for the job, and he realises that people do not take to him, and laugh at him behind his back. He has had to travel 700 miles to his territory and then work ten or twelve hours a day to earn enough to support the lifestyle he has chosen. He has no pension and the necessity of making a profit means that employees are discarded as soon as they are no longer useful. His sons do not earn enough to support him and Linda, so he is trapped in this job, without a salary, even though he is 63 years old and exhausted. When the play opens, he has already attempted suicide. When he is told that he cannot represent the firm any more, he is unable to think rationally.

His job has meant enforced separation from his family and, because he was lonely, he has been unfaithful. This not only makes him feel guilty but has caused a permanent rift between him and his favourite son, Biff. Neither of his sons is successful, because Willy taught them to value popularity over academic success, and to think that they could be 'boss big shot in two weeks' (p. 104).

To lend substance to his dreams, Willy has told lies that portray him as well-liked and successful and, shortly before the play opens, the 'birds came home to roost' and Willy has been trapped by those lies into swallowing his pride and borrowing money from his neighbour, because he no longer receives a salary. The web of deceit he has woven means that he has nobody in whom he can confide and so he summons up his successful brother, Ben, in his imagination to endorse his plan to provide for his family in the only way he can envisage, by killing himself for the insurance money. Ironically, in the Requiem, Willy is remembered for doing things that he himself took for granted and did not value — making improvements to the house.

In *Salesman in Beijing*, Miller wrote that 'the one red line connecting everyone in the play was a love for Willy; not admiration necessarily, but a kind of visceral recognition that in his fumbling and often ridiculous way he is trying to lift up a belief in immense redeeming possibilities'.

Linda Loman

As a younger woman, Linda had '*youthful energy*' (p. 26); she dyed her hair to disguise the grey and wore a ribbon. Even in the present she is '*most often jovial*' (p. 8).

Willy remembers how she used to speak out against Biff's stealing and his roughness with the girls, and that she was '*frightened of* BEN *and angry at him*'. She voices disapproval of Ben's challenging Biff to a fight and making Willy feel that he has to 'conquer the world' (p. 67).

Linda knows what is happening to Willy and does what she can to protect him, even if it means banning her beloved son from ever visiting or writing. She is totally devoted to Willy and never reveals to him that she sees through his deceptions or is aware of his failings. She does not let him know she has found the gas pipe, nor that she knows his crashes are not accidental, nor that she is aware he is borrowing money from Charley. She does not falter in her praise when he lies about the amount he has earned and then tells the truth. She never criticises him, never makes him lose face. She always encourages him to think that next week he will do better. Willy says that Linda is his 'foundation' and 'support' (p. 13), she is 'the best there is', 'a pal' (p. 29), and he is lonely without her as he travels. Linda '*more than loves* [Willy], *she admires him*' (p. 8).

As he lapses into depression, Linda coaxes him out of it by telling him he does not talk too much, he is just lively. Willy's memories may distort the facts but they enable us to see how Linda supported Willy so that he could bring up a family who love him, support them in relative comfort and pay off the mortgage on a house. With hindsight we can criticise her for encouraging his false dreams and making excuses for him. However, in the stage directions, we are told that she shares his '*turbulent longings…but lacks the temperament to utter and follow to their end*' (p. 8). Linda has always been the practical one, managing the finances, making ends meet and keeping the family in touch with reality.

Linda appears at first to be the stereotypical patient, submissive wife but Miller gradually reveals her strength. She is the emotional core of the family, and it is the unifying force of her love that holds it together. It is not only Willy who needs her. Biff adores his mother, always leaping to her defence when he thinks she is not being treated with respect, and he is prepared to stay in New York, a city he hates, to please her. Happy is searching for a woman like her, 'Somebody with character, with resistance! Like Mom, y'know?' (p. 19). When she turns on them in anger, she is formidable, frightening Happy and reducing Biff to self-

Context

In *Timebends*, Miller describes his uncle's wife as the one who 'bore the cross for them all', by 'keeping up her calm enthusiastic smile lest he feel he was not being appreciated'.

Context

In a 1987 interview, Miller said: 'Linda sustains the illusion because that's the only way Willy can be sustained…any cure or change is impossible in Willy. Ironically she's helping to guarantee that Willy will never recover from his illusion. She has to support it; she has no alternative, given his nature and hers.'

Context

Miller wrote: 'of course she's [Linda] a woman of that particular era…a silent, behind-the-scenes controller…I regard Linda as very admirable' (*Michigan Quarterly Review*, 1998)

Write a scene in which Linda visits a doctor for advice about Willy's deteriorating state of mind. Try to build upon Miller's presentation of her character and echo specific aspects of his form, structure and language. Write a brief commentary to accompany your new text that explains how and where you have tried to reflect the original play.

Context

Miller wrote that Biff was based on his cousin Buddy. Like Buddy, Biff is a sports hero, popular with the girls, who never made it to college because he failed to study (*Timebends*).

Taking it ▶
Further

Tennessee Williams's *Cat on a Hot Tin Roof* also features a fallen sporting idol who finds life in the real world problematic. A study of the ways in which Miller and Williams present the characters of Biff Loman and Brick Pollitt would make an excellent comparative coursework assignment.

loathing. Miller uses a metallic metaphor to emphasise her strength when he says '*she has developed an iron repression of her exceptions to WILLY's behaviour*' (p. 8). It is her love for him that gives her this strength.

She even seems to believe his stories about his popularity and about being promised a partnership by old man Wagner. When he does reveal that he knows people do not like him, she tries to cheer him by telling him he is 'doing wonderful', he is 'just lively', and he is 'the handsomest man in the world' (pp. 28, 29). Willy's acknowledgement that Linda is his 'foundation and…support' provides the key to their relationship. He is the one with the dreams while she is the one who enables him to function, keeps him in touch with reality and tries to provide rational explanations of his behaviour to calm his fears. However, she never manages to convince him that she loves him just the way he is and that he does not need to impress her.

Biff Loman

As a schoolboy, Biff was exceptionally talented at football, and this made him popular with his schoolmates. He was captain of the team for a particularly prestigious match and gloried in his success. He adored both his parents and admired his father, believing all Willy's exaggerated stories. He even planned to take off his helmet during the match and break through for a touchdown in front of 80,000 people as some kind of homage to Willy.

Willy tells Biff and Happy, 'I thank Almighty God you're both built like Adonises' (p. 25), and this direct reference to Greek mythology directs us towards the way in which Miller has used the Adonis myth. Adonis was a gorgeous child who, without any effort on his part, was loved by the goddesses Aphrodite and Persephone, just as Biff is adored by 'a crowd of girls' at school (p. 24). Adonis went hunting when he was an adolescent and was killed by a boar, and the myth says that each year he returns to where his body is buried to be killed again. When Biff was an adolescent, he went to Boston, saw his father with another woman and, as Bernard tells Willy, 'he'd given up on life' (p. 74). Each spring he returns home to try to make a success of his life, but each year he fights with his father and gives up on life again.

Biff's popularity and success at sport encouraged unpleasant characteristics: he cheated in exams, was rough with the girls, arrogant and domineering to his friends, disrespectful to his teachers and in trouble with security guards for stealing. As a boy, Willy told him to steal materials from building sites and laughed when he 'borrowed' a ball, but at 34 he should know better. He stole himself 'out of every good job since high school' (p. 104). His thefts could be subconscious acts giving him an excuse not to go back because he does not want an office job or, alternatively, psychologists explain theft as a form of love substitute, and it does seem that he became a compulsive thief only after his alienation from his father.

Since he surprised his father with the woman in Boston, there has been considerable tension between them. He abandoned his academic hopes, tried a variety of jobs and correspondence courses, but could not stick at anything. Eventually, when he was 24, Willy threw him out of the house and Biff went west, where he has been working as a ranch hand. This is the life he loves but, every spring, he grows restless and the old dream of being successful surfaces and makes him go home to his parents. His confusion is neatly revealed when he tells Happy, 'We should be mixing cement on some open plain' (p. 48). He wants the outdoor life but he cannot let go of the city.

At the beginning of the play, he tells Happy, 'I'm mixed up very bad…I'm not married, I'm not in business, I just — I'm like a boy' (p. 17). Miller tells us he is unhappy because he is '*lost*' (p. 14): he is torn between nature and nurture. His nature is to live the rural life but he has learned Willy's values of striving for success and not wasting his life. The events of the 24 hours covered by the play help him to emerge from this state of arrested development and to accept the blame for his own failure and for what is happening to his father.

Biff's turning point comes in Oliver's office building, where he suddenly realises that he can be happy if only he can accept the truth about himself. From that point on he demands and tells the truth, except for being pressured to lie to Willy in the restaurant. In the restaurant, Biff is '*strangely unnerved*' (p. 81). His meeting with Oliver has brought him face to face with the awareness that his whole life has been a 'ridiculous lie' and that he even believed the lies himself. He speaks '*with great tension and wonder*' (p. 82), because he has been forced to face the fact that he is a compulsive thief. '*Agonized*', he tells Happy that he does not know why he took the pen.

Biff runs out of the restaurant in agony, '*ready to weep*' (p. 91), because he is convinced that he can do nothing to help his father. He has realised that, instead of a 'phony little fake' (p. 95), his father is actually a 'prince', 'always for his boys' (p. 90), and he reaches out to Happy for help. He realises that the only thing that can help his father is for one of his sons to earn enough to support their parents, and he has learned that he will never be able to do this.

Context

In his *Poetics,* Aristotle set out three unities as rules for the theatre:
- Unity of time: The action of *Salesman* takes place within 24 hours.
- Unity of action: The play is concerned solely with Willy, with no subplots.
- Unity of place: Could we say that, except for the Requiem, the action is in one place — Willy's head?

Task 7

Improvisation: in groups, 'hot seat' the student who has been reading or acting Biff's part, making him answer your questions in character.

Harold Loman (Happy)

Happy has achieved a stake in society. He has a steady job, an apartment, a car and is attractive to women, but still he is lonely. Although he is 'one of the two assistants to the assistant' buyer, he claims to be the assistant buyer and dreams of becoming merchandise manager (p. 104). Linda contemptuously calls him 'a philandering bum' (p. 45). He is a compulsive womaniser, yet, although he enjoys women and gets a kick out of 'ruining' the fiancées of his superiors, he is '*lost*', searching for the woman who will resist him, a woman like his mother. Linda also calls him 'My baby', suggesting that she may be partly responsible for his immaturity (p. 45). Miller suggests his insecurity when, even though he is in his bedroom talking to his brother, stage directions say that he combs his hair and '*tries on his new hat*' (p. 19).

Miller shows us Happy in action, smoothly pretending to be a champagne salesman to give him an excuse to buy a girl a drink, and nonchalantly letting slip the lie that he trained at West Point. Like Biff, he has grown up with distorted morals: he hates himself for taking bribes and 'ruining' young women, but he admits that he loves it. He blames others for what he knows is his immoral behaviour, telling Biff, 'everybody around me is so false that I'm constantly lowering my ideals' (p. 18).

He is attracted by Biff's dream of buying a ranch together but he has inherited Willy's dreams and, to him, success is walking into the store and having 'the waves part in front of him' (p. 18), as they do for the merchandise manager because he earns $52,000. Happy has always lived in Biff's shadow, desperately trying to get attention as a boy by claiming that he was losing weight. He does not seem to have resented this, however, as his affection for and admiration of Biff are genuine. As an adult, his repeated plea for attention is that he is getting married.

When Happy declares that Willy had a good dream, 'He fought it out here, and this is where I'm gonna win it for him', it seems that he has learned nothing from Willy's death (p. 111). However, another interpretation could be that he plans to pay tribute to his father by proving that his dream was the right one. If this means that he will stop 'philandering' and put his energies into building a career, as Bernard has, then maybe Willy's death has given him the determination he needed.

Happy is well-meaning and undervalued. The way he talks about Willy's condition suggests that he is around quite frequently, and he is the son who comes downstairs to help Willy (p. 32). We know he drove into

Task 8

Write another scene for the play in which Happy tries to explain to Charley why he denied his father and walked out of the restaurant. Build upon Miller's presentation of his character and echo specific aspects of his form, structure and language. To accompany your new text, write a brief commentary that explains how and where you have tried to reflect the original play.

Context

$52,000 would be worth approximately $500,000 now.

town with his father the previous week. He has just paid for his parents to take a vacation in Florida, and he gave them money at Christmas. When Biff compares Willy unfavourably with Charley, Happy defends Willy, and when Willy finally realises that Biff loves him, Happy is '*deeply moved*' and reassures him (p. 106). Presumably he believes Willy's boasting about how successful he is and does not realise how bad the financial situation is until Linda tells them in Act One. However, he does spend money recklessly on champagne, double whiskies, etc., even after Linda has just told him that Willy has to borrow money from Charley and pretend it is his pay.

Uncle Ben

Ben, Willy's older brother, appears only in Willy's imagination. Willy thinks of him as 'a stolid man, in his sixties, with a moustache and an authoritative air. He is utterly certain of his destiny, and there is an aura of far places about him' (p. 34). It is never made clear how much older than Willy he is but it seems likely that Miller expects the actor to be the age Ben would have been in real time if he were still alive. As Willy tries to make sense of his life, he thinks the one big mistake he made was not to go to Alaska, and so he keeps thinking of the time when Ben visited and imagining him visiting again.

Willy does tell Charley that they have recently heard from Ben's wife in Africa that he died, leaving seven sons. Seven is a number frequently used in fairy tales, so it may be that this detail is imaginary as well, exaggerating Ben's dynastic family. Willy tells Charley, 'There's just one opportunity I had with that man' (p. 35), so it seems that Willy's perception of Ben is all based on one visit when Ben was on his way to Alaska, offering Willy a job there, and giving him a diamond fob watch. Linda was '*frightened*' by him, presumably because he was a bad influence on Willy and encouraged Biff to fight, teaching him 'Never fight fair with a stranger' (p. 38). However, how much of this is in Willy's imagination it is impossible to tell since we do not know when Ben actually visited.

Ben's message is that you can succeed only if you fight, but Willy idolises Ben because he is 'success incarnate' (p. 32), and he seems to be not so much a person as the embodiment of Willy's dreams. Ben appears not only in memory scenes but also in the present action at the end of Act Two, when Willy discusses with him his plan to commit suicide. He talks in a very stilted way, suggesting that Willy has memorised a few of Ben's utterances and keeps repeating them. On p. 40, Miller says he speaks giving '*great weight to each word, and with a certain vicious*

Task 9

Write a scene in which Biff and Happy talk after the funeral. Try to build upon Miller's presentation of their characters and echo specific aspects of his form, structure and language. Write a brief commentary to accompany your new text that explains how and where you have tried to reflect the original play.

Ben…seems to be not so much a person as the embodiment of Willy's dreams

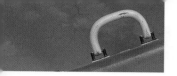

audacity', reinforcing Willy's impression that you need to be ruthless and courageous to become a success.

Willy imagines, or possibly remembers, Ben telling him he is 'first-rate' with his boys, even though Willy has just sent them to steal building materials (p. 40). When Charley warns that the jails are full of 'fearless characters', Ben adds 'And the stock exchange, friend!', '*with a laugh at* CHARLEY' (p. 39). The laugh does not indicate that he is joking but that he thinks Charley is naïve. He believes that the financial world is also like a jungle and to succeed in business you need the same ruthless competitiveness. Through Ben, Miller has demonstrated the failings of the American Dream. In the 'Wild West', the laws of the Eastern Seaboard were difficult to enforce, and the law of the jungle prevailed. Now that the West is populated, it seems that the same qualities ensure success in the East.

Charley

Through Charley, Miller refutes this version of the American Dream. Charley is a man of integrity and compassion yet still achieves success in business and raises a son who is everything Willy wants in his own sons. Charley and Ben seem like the Good and Bad Angels in a morality play, both standing on stage trying to influence Willy, who listens only to the Tempter.

Charley '*is a large man, slow of speech, laconic, immovable*', a total contrast to the volatile, irascible, insecure Willy. Willy thinks only of himself and his family, whereas Charley's '*pity, and...trepidation*' are obviously felt for Willy (p. 32). He is described in the stage directions as wearing knickerbockers, loose knee trousers like plus-fours, which helps to present him as rather old-fashioned and careless about his self-image.

Charley is a quietly successful businessman but he cannot handle tools, so Willy despises him even while he is jealous of Charley's business success. Charley cannot resist teasing Willy because he rises to the bait so easily, shouting and even challenging Charley to fist-fights. They have been neighbours a long time and Charley has always been there to help. In Willy's memory, Charley warns Willy about the dangers of sending the boys to steal building materials and he teases Willy in the hope that he will 'grow up' and see things in perspective. He has always seen through Willy's boasting, but his sarcasm is lost on Willy.

In the present, when Willy gets upset, Charley hears and comes through in his pyjamas to try to keep Willy in touch with reality, offering to

Charley and Ben seem like the Good and Bad Angels in a morality play

play cards and giving up only when Willy is abusive and not able to concentrate on the game. It is ironic that Willy has spent his whole life trying to be well liked, but not appreciating the one true friend he has until it is too late and he has already decided to kill himself.

Charley stands as a contradiction to all Willy believes in and that is why Willy cannot accept a job in Charley's firm. Charley knows himself and has no need for outward trappings of success: he still lives in the little, overshadowed house where he was living when he built up his business. He does not care about being 'well-liked', cynically telling Willy that rich men are popular because of their wealth. He claims that he did not take a strong personal interest in his son, 'My salvation is that I never took any interest in anything' (p. 75), yet Bernard is successful.

Not until Willy refuses his offer of a job for the third time does Charley show any anger. He says it is because he thinks Willy has been jealous of him all his life, but perhaps he is frustrated at Willy's stubbornness.

Bernard

Bernard is '*earnest and loyal*' (p. 24) but, in the past, he was the butt of Willy's contempt. Willy calls him 'anaemic', 'pest', 'worm'. Although younger than Biff, he is taking the same exams and Willy expects him to give Biff the answers. He is in Biff's shadow, begging to carry something so that he can be admitted to the locker room. He is described as wearing '*knickers*'. Young boys used to wear shorts in summer and knickerbockers in winter, then, at the onset of puberty, they graduated to long trousers, and this transition was a major rite of passage. This detail makes Bernard look like a sissy.

In the present, Bernard is married with two children, is a successful lawyer and has rich friends with their own tennis court. Bernard is a sensitive young man and does not want to hurt Willy, so, before he tells what he knows, he asks Willy whether he wants to talk 'candidly' (p. 73). He tells Willy that he had loved and admired Biff even though he knew Biff was taking advantage of him. As he speaks, we realise that, although not as skilled as Biff at football, Bernard was certainly no 'worm'. When Biff returned from Boston, the two boys fought for more than half an hour, seemingly evenly matched. Bernard asks Willy what happened in Boston to make Biff give up his life. When Willy grows angry, Bernard tries to calm him down and gives him good advice: 'Willy, it's better for a man just to walk away' (p. 75). The 'anaemic' 'worm' has grown into a modest, but successful and '*self-assured*' young man, contrasting strongly with Willy's two sons.

Taking it
Further

Check out the scene when Willy and Charley play cards. Go to www.youtube. com and search for 'Death Salesman Ben obsession'.

Context

Miller described his relationship with his cousin Buddy as similar to Bernard's relationship with Biff. He wrote of his uncle, Manny Newman, 'As fanatic as I was about sports, my ability was not to be compared to his sons. Since I was gangling and unhandsome, I lacked their promise. When I stopped by I always had to expect some kind of insinuation of my entire life's probable failure' (*Timebends*).

Taking it ▶
Further
. . . .
Check out a photograph
of Bing Crosby with an
Ampex 200 wire-recording
machine in 1948 at http://
tinyurl.com/38wmq46.
. . . .

Taking it ▶
Further
. . . .
Check out Dustin Hoffman
in the interview with
Howard. Go to www.
youtube.com and search
for 'Firing senior workers in
the 1940s'.
. . . .

Minor characters

Howard Wagner

Critics often classify Howard as the uncaring face of capitalism, but he is not merely a stereotype, and his role in the play is more complex than that. Howard is like Willy when a young father in that he is immensely proud of his children and abrupt with his wife. He boasts that his daughter is 'crazy' for him, just as Willy remembers his sons idolising him.

Howard always has to have the latest technological gadget and he plans to throw out his camera and his bandsaw and concentrate on the wire-recording machine. He is so out of touch with the amount his employees earn that he tells Willy that it costs 'only' $150. He is so engrossed in the machine that it is a long while before he remembers that Willy should be in Boston and asks, 'You didn't crack up again, did you?' (p. 61). Surely, a ruthless capitalist would not have let Willy continue to represent the company even though he has already 'cracked up' at least once.

Howard listens to Willy's tirade without looking at him. Even though Willy has been speaking *'angrily'* and *'banging his hand on the desk'* (pp. 63, 64), all Howard does is excuse himself politely and walk out of the room. Willy 'cracks up' again when he accidentally switches on the wire-recording machine, and he leaps away in fright, shouting. Howard gently suggests that he cannot represent the company any more because he needs a long rest, offering to review Willy's position when he feels better. Howard has believed Willy's boasts about how successful his sons are, and he assumes that they will look after him. Willy grasps Howard's arm in desperation, but Howard, *'keeping himself under control'* (p. 66), leaves the room.

Nevertheless, even though Willy has completed 36 years' service with the company, Howard sacks him, and he does not even go to the funeral. Willy was abandoned by his father, then by his older brother Ben, and now by the son of the man he believes told him he would one day be a member of the firm.

The Woman

The Woman is the secretary to whom salesmen apply to meet the buyers. Although Willy tells Biff that she is called Miss Francis, Miller calls her '*The* WOMAN' throughout, even in the cast list. Her identity is not important, only her role in the plot and Willy's guilt as he remembers her. She is *'quite proper-looking,* WILLY's *age'* (p. 29), so not a prostitute but someone who makes him feel good about himself by insisting that she chose him and by telling him he is a wonderful man. She appreciates Willy's sense of humour and is happy to have 'a good time' with Willy. Their relationship is mutually beneficial: she will put him straight through to the buyers and he will give her stockings, which were expensive in the 1940s.

Her laughter is important in the play because it signals that Willy is thinking about her. Miller shows that she is a cheerful, friendly woman who is no threat to Linda and is actually good for Willy. She boosts his ego and gives him company during his long absences from home. She expects respect but not commitment. She is angry and humiliated by his denial of her and his attempt to push her out into the corridor in her underwear, and that is why she demands her stockings.

Stanley

The young waiter works hard to ingratiate himself with Happy, who is a regular customer and presumably tips well. He tells Happy, 'It's a dog's life. I only wish during the war they'd a took me in the Army. I coulda been dead by now' (p. 78), but Miller does not reveal why he is so depressed. He tells Happy about the dishonest bartender but he is obviously loyal to his colleagues and has not told his boss.

When Happy and Biff walk out, leaving their father in the washroom, Stanley calls after Happy '*indignantly*' (p. 91). When Willy is '*left on the floor on his knees*' (p. 95) poignantly calling Biff to come back, it is Stanley who '*helps* WILLY *to his feet*'. He helps to make Willy feel better about himself by flicking '*a speck off* WILLY'*s lapel*' (p. 96) and unobtrusively returns the tip Willy gives him. Stanley watches him leave and rebukes the waiter who is staring at Willy.

Stanley has a small but crucial role in the play. Miller presents him as a strong contrast to Willy's sons. Stanley owes nothing to Willy, but he is compassionate, considerate and honest. He has had a hard life, and he has a menial job, but he does it well and is loyal to his colleagues.

> Stanley has a small but crucial role in the play.

Off-stage characters

Willy's father

When Willy thinks of his father, this is signalled by the sound of the flute, which tells of '*grass and trees and the horizon*'. He made his living by making and selling flutes as the family travelled across the continent. We are never told why he deserted his family before Willy was four,

but this explains why Willy still feels 'kind of temporary' (p. 40). He has inherited his father's pioneering spirit but, instead of opening up undiscovered territory and selling something he has made himself, Willy has spent his life opening up territories as a salesman for someone else. He has inherited his father's practical ability, but the urban version of the American Dream to which he aspires does not value these skills.

Dave Singleman

As his name suggests, Singleman is unique: he is a legendary salesman who gives substance to Willy's dream, convincing him that 'selling was the greatest career a man could want' (p. 63). Willy views him as a success because, even at the age of 84, he was still able to sell his wares by telephone and was so popular that hundreds of buyers and salesmen attended his funeral. Willy does not seem to realise that Singleman may not have been that successful if he still had to travel hundreds of miles to earn a living at the age of 84. Willy remembers that he did not go to Alaska because he had met this man. He was encouraged to persevere as a salesman, believing that he too would have hundreds of mourners at his funeral. Whereas Ben represents the opportunity to get rich, Singleman represents the aspect of the American Dream that emphasises the importance of being 'well-liked'.

Mr Birnbaum

Willy blames Mr Birnbaum for Biff's failure, telling Bernard, 'that son-of-a-bitch ruined his life' (p. 73), rather than face up to the fact that Biff gave up his academic ambitions after he found his father with another woman. Mr Birnbaum demonstrated that for Biff to be 'well-liked' was not enough — he also needed to work. Biff interprets his own failure as an act of spite by Mr Birnbaum because he had once exposed the teacher to ridicule in front of the class. However, in a public exam there is no opportunity for tinkering with the marks. The fact that the maths teacher warned him that, if he continued to miss maths lessons for football practice, he would fail the Regents' exam, suggests that he was actually being very fair.

Form, structure and language

This section is designed to offer you information about the three strands of AO2 (see p. 80 of this guide). This Assessment Objective requires you to demonstrate detailed critical understanding in analysing the ways in which form, structure and language shape meanings in literary texts.

To a certain extent these three terms should, as indicated elsewhere, be seen as fluid and interactive. Remember, however, that in the analysis of a play such as *Death of a Salesman*, aspects of form and structure are at least as important as language. You should certainly not focus your study merely on lexical features of the text. Many features of form, structure and language in *Death of a Salesman* are further explored elsewhere in this book in the act summaries and in exemplar essays.

Form and genre

Stage play

In a stage play, the set, lighting and sound effects are of crucial importance and Miller has described precisely how he wants the play to be staged. The original title of this play was *The Inside of His Head* and, since Miller wants us to see the workings of Willy's mind, the set is constructed to enable the audience to see both the objective reality and what Willy believes is happening. Miller's original stage image was of a large head opening to reveal a 'mass of contradictions', and he has cleverly suggested this in a subtle combination of sound, lighting and set design.

Before the curtain rises, the audience hears a small, fine flute melody that suggests wide open spaces. This impression, however, is soon contradicted by the set with its '*towering, angular shapes*', dwarfing the little house, and the '*angry*' glow of orange in the sky, creating a mood that suggests anger at being hemmed in, caged by buildings. The flute music speaks of the past, reminding the audience of the Dream of the Founding Fathers, whereas the '*hard towers of the apartment buildings*'

Context

In the introduction to *Collected Plays*, 1957, Miller wrote: 'the first image that occurred to me... was of an enormous face, the height of the proscenium arch, which would appear and then open up, and we would see the inside of a man's head.'

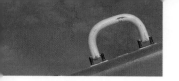

symbolise the materialism that has corrupted the Dream in the modern world. Willy complains that the 'Population is getting out of control' (p. 12), but his living depends on having an increasing population to buy goods, and these people need homes. Apartment blocks were built to house them, turning semi-rural Brooklyn into an integral part of the city of New York. In Willy's little house, overshadowed by apartment blocks, Miller has provided a graphic image of how the commercialisation of the American Dream has destroyed its roots.

Part of the stage set from the original Broadway production (c. 1949), showing the kitchen, stairs and upper bedroom; the other bedroom is to the left of the picture

Condé Nast Archive/Corbis

Miller tells us that '*The air of a dream clings to the place*'

Miller tells us that '*The air of a dream clings to the place*', but he describes a realistic set. Two bedrooms, a staircase, and the kitchen should be visible simultaneously, although the living-room is unseen. The set should comprise a kitchen table, three chairs and a refrigerator, but no other fixtures. The table and chairs symbolise family life, but one chair is missing — possibly Miller just wants to keep the stage clear for action, but it also serves as a reminder that Biff was thrown out of the house by Willy and rarely returns. In 1948, most people did not have a refrigerator and so Miller is drawing attention to Willy's material success. In the original production, Mielziner was careful to use objects that were very obviously lower middle class. They were battered as if the Lomans actually owned and used them. Miller also specifies that a silver athletic trophy, presumably Biff's, stands on the shelf above Willy's and Linda's bed, symbolising the way Willy idolises Biff and has transferred his dreams on to his son.

Miller's stage directions are often impossible to enact on stage but act as reminders to the actors. How, for instance, is the actor to suggest that Willy hears the flute but is not aware of it? Miller is signalling that it is important for the actor to be aware that Willy's dream is present in his subconscious even when he is not actually thinking about it.

The flute fades away soon after Willy's entrance and then, later, '*He breaks off in amazement and fright as the flute is heard distantly*' (p. 13). The flute melody is a signal that Willy's mind is drifting into the past: he breaks off because he realises that his mind is confusing past and present. Miller also uses lighting to suggest time, as well as to direct the audience's attention to the appropriate part of the set. When Willy's mind drifts into his memories, the apartment houses fade away '*and the entire house and its surroundings become covered with leaves*' (p. 21), indicating that, inside Willy's head, he is back in the past, before the trees were cut down to build apartments. As the leaves appear, '*music insinuates itself*', a description that suggests the gentle pastoral flute music which accompanies happy thoughts.

The walls of the house are carefully respected by the actors during the scenes in the present, but in Willy's reminiscences they disappear and the actors speak and walk through them. Scenes set in other places are played out on the forestage so that the audience can simultaneously watch what is happening in the present and in Willy's mind.

At the end of Act One, the characters are speaking optimistically but the stage directions direct the audience to believe that their hopes are unfounded. 'BIFF *enters the darkened kitchen, takes a cigarette and… comes downstage into a golden pool of light*' (p. 54). We have seen enough of Biff to realise that the golden pool of light that illuminates him is ironic, suggesting the falseness of Willy's dream of greatness for him. The light on Willy and Linda's bedroom fades so that the audience's attention is drawn to the gas heater, which '*begins to glow through the kitchen wall…a blue flame beneath red coils*'. This reminds the audience of Willy's suicidal thoughts.

Biff stares at the heater, reaches behind it and removes the tubing, '*horrified*', which suggests that he may have accepted responsibility for his father, although this action foreshadows a brutal confrontation later. As Willy talks hopefully of the next day, Linda starts humming a soft lullaby to relax him. Gradually this humming becomes '*desperate but

Context

Miller wrote that Mielziner's set was 'an emblem of Willy's intense longing for the promises of the past, with which…the present state of his mind is always conflicting, and it was thus both a lyrical design and a dramatic one' (*Timebends*).

Taking it ▶ **Further**

Go to www.neh.gov/ whoweare and look at Mielziner's sketch for a set design by clicking on Awards / Arthur Miller / Appreciation.

Context

Miller wrote: 'how wonderful, I thought, to do a play without transitions at all, dialogue that would simply leap from bone to bone of a skeleton that would not for an instant cease being added to, an organism as strictly economic as a leaf, as trim as an ant' (*Timebends*).

Context

Miller wrote that 'the chair must become alive, quite as though his old boss were in it as he addresses him'. In the first production, 'rather than being lit, the chair subtly seemed to begin emanating light' (*Timebends*).

monotonous' (p. 54), creating an ominous mood of fear, and unsettling the audience for the interval.

Nevertheless, gay, bright music, evoking optimism, fades away as the curtain rises on Act Two. Willy approaches Howard diffidently but hopefully, and Miller cleverly uses the wire-recording machine to unnerve him. 'On HOWARD's *exit, the light on his chair grows very bright and strange*' (p. 64). The stage directions specify that '*the light…occupies the chair, animating it*', helping to dramatise what is going on inside Willy's head without actually bringing another character on stage.

As Howard leaves, '[BEN's] *music is heard — first distantly, then closer,*' (p. 66) so that we can feel how Willy drifts slowly into the world of his imagination. Miller has not specified the type of music needed to accompany thoughts of Ben, but it should help to convey '*an aura of far places*' and that '*he is utterly certain of his destiny*' (p. 34).

'*Raucous music*' suggests the brash type of restaurant Happy has chosen for the family meal, and the '*red glow*' adds to the impression that the '*lavishly dressed*' Miss Forsythe and Letta are prostitutes (pp. 78, 79). If this is where Happy seeks female companionship, it is not surprising that he has not yet met a girl like his mother. The music has stopped by the time Biff starts to tell Willy about his meeting with Oliver, and the '*silence*' raises the tension as Biff, '*high, slightly alcoholic, above the earth*' tries to speak, and '*his breath keeps breaking the rhythm of his voice*' (p. 84). As Biff attempts to 'hold on to the facts' and Willy refuses to listen to them, they both grow angry, and '*A single trumpet note jars the ear*' (p. 86). With this simple theatrical device, Miller signals that, instead of Willy drifting into the past, he is painfully thrust back into his repressed memory.

First, however, Willy reconstructs in his imagination a scene at which he was not present, when Bernard told Linda that Biff had failed maths and caught a train to Boston. This scene is enacted in the house behind the restaurant table, which is on the forestage, so we are aware of the present action at the same time as we watch Willy's thoughts being enacted in the house with '*the light of green leaves*' holding '*the air of night and a dream*'(p. 86). As Willy stops listening to him, the lights fade low on the forestage and Biff continues to talk inaudibly. As Willy comes back to the present and the sudden realisation that Biff stole Oliver's pen, the '*light on house area snaps out*' (p. 87).

The operator's voice signals Willy's return to his imagined memory, and the woman's laugh and voice off-stage signal that he is losing his grasp on the present. Sound effects have helped the audience feel the build-up of tension, from the single trumpet note, through Bernard's

…we are aware of the present action at the same time as we watch Willy's thoughts being enacted

frantic knocking at the house, through the ringing of the telephone, the raw sensuous music, the woman laughing and the repeated knocking at the door of the hotel room. Willy, '*his terror rising*' (p. 92), pushes the woman away from him and steps away. The light follows him to Biff, and there is a sudden silence.

After the re-enactment of his repressed memory, Willy is on his knees and, as he returns to the present with Stanley's help, his theme music is heard and his thoughts turn to the outdoors and planting seeds. Miller specifies flute music in the '*long pause*' before the next scene while the audience waits to see what will happen next.

When we catch up with Willy on the forestage, planting seeds, '*He is in the blue of night*' (p. 99), a direction that suggests sadness as well as darkness. Ben voices Willy's fear that Biff will hate him, and '*the gay music of the boys is heard*' (p. 101) as Willy remembers the wonderful relationship he had with his sons before the fateful day in Boston. When Biff breaks down and Willy realises that his son loves him, '*In accents of dread,* BEN'S *idyllic music starts up*' (p. 106). This confident music must be played in such a way that the audience can sense the dreadful way Willy's mind is working but, as Ben goes and his music fades, Willy has lost his confidence and his mind is in turmoil:

> *He turns around as if to find his way; sounds, faces, voices, seem to be swarming in upon him and he flicks at them, crying, 'Sh! Sh!' Suddenly music, faint and high, stops him. It rises in intensity, almost to an unbearable scream. He goes up and down on his toes, and rushes off around the house.* (p. 108)

The rest of the story is told in music and mime as, once '*the music crashes down in a frenzy of sound*' signifying the car crash, it becomes '*the soft pulsation of a single 'cello string*' then develops '*into a dead march. The leaves of day are appearing over everything*' as the mourners gather at Willy's graveside (p. 108). At the end of the Requiem, the flute music accompanies Linda's final speech and, as the mourners leave the stage, '*Only the music of the flute is left on the darkening stage as over the house the hard towers of the apartment buildings rise into sharp focus*' (p. 112). The audience is left with the same conflicting signals that were there as the curtain went up. Nothing has been resolved.

Motif: kneeling

When each of the three main characters finally gives up the struggle, the stage directions show them symbolically kneeling. While Willy remembers Biff sitting on his suitcase, '*motionless, tears falling*', after

Sound effects have helped the audience feel the build-up of tension.

Context

In the introduction to *Collected Plays*, 1957, Miller wrote that he wanted 'not a mounting line of tension, nor a gradually narrowing cone of intensifying suspense, but a bloc, a single chord presented as such at the outset, within which all the strains and melodies would already be contained. The strategy…was to appear entirely unstrategic.'

finding his father with another woman, Willy kneels down beside him, as if to expiate his sin (p. 94). When he finally confronts this memory, he is in the restaurant, 'on his knees', and it is Stanley, a stranger, who helps him up (p. 95).

Biff half kneels to his father on one knee in the restaurant when he is shocked and horrified by Willy's state of mind, accepting his responsibility and promising to 'make good'. However, he gets down on both knees to pick up the flowers Linda so contemptuously knocked to the floor, and he stays there, in front of Linda, filled with '*self-loathing*' by her angry accusations (p. 98).

At the funeral, Linda, who has supported Willy so strongly throughout, is finally on her knees. Miller offers a symbolic suggestion of hope because it is Biff who '*lifts her to her feet and moves out up right with her in his arms*' (p. 112), suggesting that he is no longer the 'boy' he felt like at the beginning, but that he has grown up and accepted his responsibilities as a member of a family.

Tragedy

The word 'tragedy' comes from the Greek words for 'goat' and 'song', and it could well be argued that Miller has presented Willy Loman as a scapegoat or sacrifice to American capitalism. The Greek playwright Aristotle defined a tragic hero as a man of noble stature who has a fatal flaw or suffers an error of judgement that leads to his downfall. The suffering is not wholly deserved and through that suffering the character gains some self-awareness that turns his defeat into a sort of triumph.

Although Willy is not noble, he believes he is special. Miller might be attempting to enhance his tragic stature when Biff calls him 'A hard-working, unappreciated prince' (p. 90), and perhaps his '*massive dreams*' help to suggest that he is heroic. His fatal flaw could be said to be self-deception, arising out of his lack of confidence. He brings his fate upon himself by betraying Linda, but few would condemn him to death for adultery. Linda compares Willy to 'a little boat looking for a harbour' (p. 59) because he is vulnerable to the vicissitudes of American society, just as a boat is vulnerable to the elements.

With the loss of his dreams of success, Willy's life has lost its meaning for him and he seeks to fulfil his dreams and find a meaning in his death. For a theatre audience, his tragic stature is enhanced when he is honest to himself and to Linda, because these admissions reveal that he can distinguish between his dreams and reality. Deep down he does know himself, even while he strives to be thought of as something greater.

However, Aristotle also points out that the most important element of a tragedy is not a tragic hero but 'the arrangement of the incidents, for tragedy is an imitation, not of men but of action and life, of happiness and misfortune'. It is in the form Miller has chosen that he is able to expose the lack of meaning in Willy's life and, indeed, in his death. It could be said that the tragedy is in the fact that he had the wrong dreams and that, without them, he could have been happy with his loving family. It is not the protagonist who gains self-awareness that turns his defeat into a sort of triumph, but the audience members who are forced to think about what they value in life.

According to Aristotle, a tragedy should not leave the audience feeling depressed but rather with a sense of *catharsis*, the emotional cleansing brought about by an extreme change in emotion resulting from strong feelings of sorrow, fear or pity. The first time I saw *Death of a Salesman* was at Nottingham Playhouse in 1967, with John Neville as Willy Loman. At the end of the play, the audience was stunned into silence, emptied of emotion, and it took a while for us to collect our senses and applaud a mesmerising performance.

For me, therefore, the play is definitely a tragedy, but perhaps there is no tragic hero. Biff is the character who promises greatness at the beginning of the story, and the one who gains the self-awareness that could be said to turn defeat into a sort of triumph. In another form, Biff might have been the hero, but in this play Miller is concerned to explore the inside of Willy's head, and Biff, although important, is a supporting character.

Willy's failings are ones we can recognise. We all desire to be liked by many and loved by our families. It is human nature to dream of success for ourselves and our children, and parents do tend to look to themselves for explanations of why their children have not lived up to their expectations. The play demonstrates how these natural human weaknesses can destroy a man as surely as those major faults that lead to the deaths of Shakespeare's tragic heroes. Nevertheless, it is not Willy's failings alone that lead to his death, but also the false promises of the American Dream.

Comedy

In the *Michigan Quarterly Review*, Miller wrote that he:

> **...wanted a form that could sustain in itself the way we deal with crises, which is not to deal with them. After all, there**

> **Context**
>
> In *Tragedy and the Common Man* (1949) Miller wrote 'I believe that the common man is as apt a subject for tragedy in its highest sense as kings were…'

> **Context**
>
> Miller wrote: 'we are in the presence of a character who is ready to lay down his life, if need be, to secure one thing — his sense of personal dignity' (*Tragedy and the Common Man*, 1949).

is a lot of comedy in *Salesman*; people forget it because it is so dark by the end of the play. But if you stand behind the audience you hear a lot of laughter. It's a deadly ironical laughter most of the time, but it *is* a species of comedy. The comedy is really a way for Willy and others to put off the evil day, which is the thing we all do. I wanted that to *happen* and not be something talked *about*. (1985)

Psychomachia

psychomachia
conflict in the soul

The subtitle to *Death of a Salesman* is: 'Certain private conversations in two acts and a requiem', presumably referring to conversations in Willy's mind and also those taking place in the present. Those private conversations that take place in his head reveal the conflict in his soul, or **psychomachia**. When he talks with his brother, Ben, who visited only once, these sequences are obviously internal conversations in which he debates his problems. When considering suicide, the imaginary Ben gives voice to Willy's doubts, saying 'They might not honour the policy' and 'It's called a cowardly thing' (p. 100). Ben then seems to yield to Willy's optimism, but he suddenly says that Biff will 'call you a coward... And a damned fool...He'll hate you, William' (pp. 100–01).

In Willy's distorted memories, it is difficult to discern the truth but it seems likely that other conversations also reflect the conflict in his own mind. For instance, when Ben offers him the job in Alaska, Willy is tempted, and in his memory it is Linda who dissuades him from going. He gives in very easily, however, suggesting that he did not need to be persuaded. Willy is tempted by the outdoor life, but his dreams lie in the city where 'a man can end up with diamonds...on the basis of being liked!' (p. 68). Because Willy was not willing to give up everything he had to follow Ben to Alaska, he emphasises the risks and the ruthless personality needed to be successful there and imagines Ben telling him 'Screw on your fists and you can fight for a fortune up there' (p. 66).

Willy admires his father and begs Ben to tell the boys about him because he wants 'them to know the kind of stock they spring from'. He thinks of his father as a 'Great inventor...With one gadget he made more in a week than a man like you could make in a lifetime' (p. 38). However, he tells Biff, 'Even your grandfather was better than a carpenter' (p. 48). Willy is full of such contradictions, which are amusing to an audience but which point to the psychomachia going on inside his head. Biff is a 'lazy bum', and at the same time he is 'such a hard worker' (p. 11). 'Chevrolet, Linda, is the greatest car ever built' (p. 26), but 'That goddam Chevrolet, they ought to prohibit the manufacture of that car!' (p. 28). When Biff goes to meet Oliver, Willy tells him 'Be quiet, fine, and serious' then advises him to 'Walk in with a big laugh' (p. 51).

The play revolves around the exploration of a man's mind as he grapples with his responsibility for others. The techniques Miller employs have to be expressionistic so that we can see inside Willy's mind to understand the conflicts and how he tries to resolve them.

> The play revolves around the exploration of a man's mind

Structure

Miller needed to create a dramatic structure that would explore the workings of Willy's mind at the same time as it allowed what was happening in the real world to be enacted, interweaving his dreams and fractured memories with the triggers that evoked them. Miller wrote in the Introduction to his *Collected Plays* that, 'I was convinced only that if I could make him remember enough he would kill himself, and the structure of the play was determined by what was needed to draw up his memories like a mass of tangled roots without end or beginning.' The play's structure is dictated by the way Willy's mind works, so it cannot be divided into neatly contained scenes, and it inevitably leads to a crisis.

Miller does not call his work a play, but 'certain private conversations in two acts and a requiem', so we are aware from the beginning that the structure is unusual. The first act gives us the information we need, introducing the main characters, establishing the unusual narrative technique of blending present reality with Willy's memory sequences, as well as dropping hints about what has happened and what will happen that will be picked up in Act Two. Act One ends on a climax of hope that is undermined by the stage directions. The second act builds to a double climax as Biff realises the truth and desperately tries to persuade Willy to accept it, and Willy, realising that Biff loves him, finally decides to kill himself for the good of the family.

The story is now complete but some loose ends need to be tied up. Miller has ironically called the final scene 'Requiem', the Catholic mass calling for the eternal rest of the dead. The five characters around the grave are not praying but they are showing respect and love. They do not look forward to a glorious afterlife but reinforce the feeling that Willy's life and his death have been meaningless. The Requiem dramatises the failure of Willy's dream of a funeral like Dave Singleman's, suggests what might happen with Willy's two sons in the future, and it points out the irony

Task **10**

Explore different possible interpretations of what Biff and Happy might do now that their father is dead, and support these possibilities with close reference to and analysis of the text.

that he kills himself on the day when Linda has successfully paid off the mortgage. This short scene focuses the audience's attention on the varying versions of the American Dream and how it has become distorted. Instead of offering opportunity, it destroys lives and relationships. More than this, however, the Requiem offers a stronger emotional impact, and it could be argued that it turns a dramatic play into a tragedy.

Language

Dialogue

Context

Miller wrote:

…it is necessary to employ the artificial in order to arrive at the real. More than one actor has told me that it is surprisingly difficult to memorize their dialogue. The speeches sound like real, almost reported talk when in fact they are intensely composed, compressed into a sequential inevitability that seems natural but isn't (*Notes on Realism, Echoes Down the Corridor*, 2000).

Task 11

Find further examples of colloquial language in the play.

Most of the time, Miller has constructed colloquial dialogue that follows the speech patterns of ordinary people living in New York. He uses slang vocabulary such as 'drummer', 'boss big shot' and 'sons-of-bitches'; clichés such as 'dime a dozen', 'the sky's the limit' and 'mountains out of molehills'; and he gives the men taboo language including 'Goddammit', 'God Almighty' and 'What the hell'. He uses abbreviations such as 'ads' and 'Chevvy', and he elides words to make sure the actors use the colloquial contracted forms of verb phrases such as 'gonna', 'coulda' and 'y'know'. Ellipsis helps to reproduce the sentence constructions of informal speech that often omit essential clause elements, for instance: 'Want one?' 'Lotta dreams and plans' and the sceptical response 'Oh, go on.' Miller also gives the characters tag questions, such as 'Funny, y'know?' and 'A pal, you understand?'

There is American vocabulary, such as 'nickel', 'dime', 'stoop', 'mail', 'ash-can', and 'flunk'. Some phrases will be unfamiliar to British English speakers. Willy says he 'Sold a nice bill' in Waterbury, presumably meaning that he made a good sale. While anticipating the match, Biff says, 'I'm takin' one play for Pop', presumably meaning that he is going to break ranks and make a touchdown in honour of his father. Willy tells Ben that all he is doing is 'ringing up a zero', comparing his life metaphorically with a cash register that has nothing put in it.

Miller also gives his characters colloquial syntax most of the time with incomplete sentences, interruptions and imperatives. The conversations are full of questions, exclamations, hesitations and repetition. The characters often use non-standard grammar such as 'There's fifty men' and 'A salesman is got to dream'. Linda, however, uses rhetorical features such as passive constructions and rhetorical questions even though her vocabulary is quite ordinary.

Willy's aspirations are revealed not in his syntax but in his occasional use of a higher register of language. Sometimes Miller gives him lyrical, poetic language such as: 'I want you to know, on the train, in the mountains, in the valleys, wherever you go, that you cut down your life for spite!' (p. 103). Willy compares his sons to 'Adonis' and 'Hercules', figures in classical mythology. He refers to well-known Americans such as B. F. Goodrich, an industrialist in the rubber industry, and Thomas Edison, a prolific inventor who developed, among many other things, the phonograph and the motion picture camera.

All the family members try to elevate the tone of their speech with high register polysyllabic Latinate vocabulary such as 'congratulate you on your initiative', 'prohibit the manufacture', 'success incarnate' (pp. 23, 28, 32). Sometimes this can sound awkward as when Willy talks about 'observing the scenery', Happy bemoans a 'crummy characteristic' and Biff uses 'contemptuous' when he means 'contemptible' (pp. 9, 19, 105).

> **Miller gives Willy lyrical, poetic language**

Imagery

The rubber hose

The rubber hose is the tangible evidence that Willy is contemplating suicide as he has put a 'new little nipple on the gas pipe' (p. 47). Linda removes the hose but she returns it before Willy comes home, because she cannot insult him by letting him know that she is aware of his intentions. Biff does not have the same concern for Willy's dignity as his mother has.

Miller said in an interview in 1987 that, 'Like many myths and classical dramas, it is a story about violence within a family.' The rubber hose is the metaphorical dagger with which Biff fatally stabs his father. With this graphic image he destroys Willy's dignity and leaves him no way of escape. Miller says that, as Willy refuses to look at it, he is '*caged, wanting to escape*' (p. 103). After this confrontation, Willy's death is inevitable.

Symbols

Miller uses many symbols to make points visually, for instance, the suitcases symbolise Willy's past, and Biff's sneakers symbolise his academic hopes.

> **Context**
>
> In the introduction to *Collected Plays,* 1957, Miller wrote: 'Any dramatic form is an artifice, a way of transforming a subjective feeling into something that can be comprehended through public symbols.'

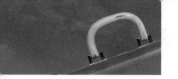

Context

Check out a 1928
Chevrolet. Go to **http://
americanhistory.si.edu**,
type '1928 Chevrolet
sedan' into the search
box and follow the link.

Cars

A car is vital to a travelling salesman as well as being symbolic of a man's material success and his freedom. In Willy's mind, the car is a proud symbol of his status, his independence and his sons' love for him. However, Willy's loss of control over his car symbolises his loss of control over his life. Ironically, the car gives him geographical mobility but it traps him and becomes the means of his destruction.

The wire-recording machine

As well as being a neat way of bringing Howard's family on stage, the wire-recording machine is a symbol of 'progress'. It is the latest gadget invented by this consumer society and Howard's latest fad, which prevents him from giving proper attention to Willy. When Willy accidentally switches the recorder on, it triggers the hysterical breakdown that demonstrates to Howard his fragile mental state and prompts Howard to fire him. Ironically, as Willy keeps trying to relive the past in an effort to understand what went wrong, this machine captures the past for eternity. It symbolises Willy's inability to cope with the modern world, and the continuous recitation draws attention to the mechanisation of the modern world and the lack of human empathy, demonstrated so poignantly when Howard urges Willy to buy one.

Taking it ▶
Further

The car is also a dominant symbol in F. Scott Fitzgerald's *The Great Gatsby*. An exploration of the way it is used in both texts would make a good study for a comparative coursework essay.

Through the medium of the recorder, we learn of Howard's pride in his children and his brusqueness with his wife, which creates a parallel with Willy. His pride in his children blinds Howard to Willy's plight and supersedes the loyalty he should have felt to his father's employee, just as Willy's pride in his sons blinded him to Bernard's worth and Charley's genuine friendship.

A jungle

Top ten *quotation* ▶

Ben boasts, 'when I was seventeen I walked into the jungle, and when I was twenty-one I walked out. And by God I was rich' (p. 37). Willy's response is, 'That's just the spirit I want to imbue them (Biff and Happy) with! To walk into a jungle!' For Willy, a jungle is a symbol of a hostile environment that offers riches to those who are prepared to take risks. When he has his imaginary conversation with Ben at the end of Act Two, Ben seems to be encouraging him to commit suicide. Death may be frightening but, 'One must go in to fetch a diamond out.' Willy missed his chance to go to Alaska but now there is another daunting jungle offering the rich prize of the insurance money: 'The jungle is dark but full of diamonds' (p. 106).

Diamonds

Diamonds become symbols of financial success. Ben gives Willy a diamond fob watch as evidence of his wealth and Willy pawns it to pay for a correspondence course for Biff, as though Ben's success will be passed on to Biff. The appointment with Oliver was illusory but Willy sees the insurance money as 'like a diamond, shining in the dark, hard and rough, that I can pick up and touch in my hand' (p. 100). A diamond represents an opportunity for a man to make a success of his life. In Willy's mind, even in New York, 'a man can end up with diamonds here on the basis of being liked' (p. 68).

Seeds

On p. 12, Willy remembers the plants that used to grow in the garden and bemoans the fact that 'you can't raise a carrot in the backyard'. Nevertheless, at the beginning of Act Two, optimistic because Biff is going to see Bill Oliver, Willy comments, 'Gee, on the way home tonight I'd like to buy some seeds', and he dreams of getting a little place in the country where he can grow vegetables. Seeds represent his yearning for the outdoor life and his hopes for the future. After he is fired from his job and his sons abandon him in the restaurant, Willy actually buys seeds and plants them, as if admitting that all his other hopes have come to nothing. He seems to be trying, too late, to re-establish the contact with nature that he used to have but which has been stifled by the city.

Seeds represent Willy's need to leave a legacy behind him. They seem to represent a realisation that his own seed, his children, will never grow into the successful men he has dreamed of. The seeds he has sown during his working life have led only to his being fired. He judges success on how 'well-liked' a man is and dreams of hundreds of people at his funeral. However not even Howard Wagner comes to his funeral, after Willy has served the firm loyally for 35 years, opening up new territories for them.

> The seeds he has sown during his working life have led only to his being fired

Ironically, it is inevitable that the real seeds he plants will come to nothing because the garden is so overshadowed by the apartment buildings, just as the insurance company will probably refuse to pay out because he has a history of suicide attempts. Willy's hopes for his boys have not grown because they are overshadowed by the materialistic values in New York. Like the seeds trapped in a sterile garden, Willy Loman is trapped in a society and a mindset that prevent him from developing into anything that will last and, just as he has blighted his own life, he has blighted the lives of his sons as well.

Stockings

Willy gives stockings to the woman in Boston, so, whenever he sees Linda mending her stockings, he is reminded of his betrayal, and his guilt makes him angry. Linda is the one who looks after the family's finances, trying to make ends meet, so she mends stockings rather than throw them away. When Willy sees her mending them, it is like an accusation that he is failing to provide for his family, so stockings become a symbol of his guilt and his shame.

PHILIP ALLAN LITERATURE GUIDE FOR A-LEVEL

Contents

This section is designed to offer you an insight into the influence of some significant contexts in which *Death of a Salesman* was written and has been performed and received. AO4 (see p. 81 of this guide) requires demonstration of an understanding of the significance of contexts of production and reception. Such contextual material should, however, be used with caution. Reference to contexts is only valuable when it genuinely informs a reading of the text. Contextual material which is clumsily introduced or 'bolted on' to an argument will contribute very little to the argument.

Biographical context

Arthur Miller was born on 17 October, 1915, into a wealthy Jewish family, who lived in an elegant apartment in Harlem, overlooking Central Park. His father, Isidore, had a successful business manufacturing coats, and he employed 1,000 workers. Isidore Miller, an illiterate Polish immigrant, seemed to have achieved the American Dream, but in the Stock Market Crash of 1929, he lost his business and his savings. The family had to move to a small house in Brooklyn and Miller had to work his way through high school and university. His mother, Augusta, had been a schoolteacher and she was disappointed because he was a poor student at school, interested only in football and athletics.

The miseries caused by the Depression had a profound effect on Miller, leaving him with a feeling of responsibility. He even joined the picket line when his own father's employees were on strike. He had a variety of temporary jobs, which gave him experience of life and introduced him to a wide range of people, both important preparations for a writer. He worked for two years in an automobile warehouse to earn the money to go to university. The University of Michigan twice rejected him to study English, but he was finally accepted, after a persuasive letter to the admissions officer, to read journalism. As well as journalism, he studied playwriting, and he became night editor of *Michigan Daily*. He was tempted to volunteer to fight against fascism in the Spanish Civil War but realised he could have more impact writing plays. In an interview with Christopher Bigsby, he said, 'I chose theatre [because] it was the cockpit of literary activity and you could talk directly to an audience and radicalize the people.' He won several awards for his plays while at university.

Taking it **Further** ▶

Watch a fascinating talk by Christopher Bigsby, telling Arthur Miller's story. Go to http://vimeo.com and search for 'Arthur Miller Bigsby'.

Taking it **Further** ▶

Check out a 2001 interview with Arthur Miller: go to www.youtube.com and search for 'Arthur Miller 2001 interview and clips'.

Miller graduated in 1938 and moved to New York, taking various odd
jobs and continuing to write plays, while his wife, Mary Slattery, was
the main breadwinner. During the war he wrote *All My Sons,* his first
successful Broadway play, but it was not produced until 1947. It was an
immediate success and he followed it with *Death of a Salesman.* He told
Christopher Bigsby that the play was about:

> ...**what happens when everybody has a refrigerator and a
> car. I wrote *Salesman* at the beginning of the greatest boom
> in world history but I felt that the reality was Depression,
> the whole thing coming down in a heap of ashes. There
> was still the feel of the Depression, the fear that everything
> would disappear.**

The Cold War between America and Russia led to a hysterical fear of
communism, which was perceived as a threat to the American way of
life. Senator Joseph McCarthy claimed that there were large numbers of
Communists as well as Soviet spies and sympathisers inside the United
States' federal government and elsewhere. During this post-Second World
War era of McCarthyism, many thousands of Americans were accused of
being Communists or Communist sympathisers and became the subject
of aggressive investigations and interrogation. Before Stanley Kramer's
film of *Salesman* was released, Miller was asked by Columbia Pictures
to place an advertisement in the theatrical trade press denouncing
communism. Miller refused. Columbia, however, released a short film of
interviews with business professors who explained that selling was an
honourable profession, and Willy was not typical.

Miller's response was to write *The Crucible* in 1953, which is a thinly
disguised criticism of this hysteria. In 1954, he was denied a passport
because of his alleged support of the Communist movement. In 1955,
he was given a contract to write a film for the New York City Youth
Board but was dropped from the film after a newspaper published a
condemnation of his leftist activities. In 1957, he was called before the
House Un-American Activities Committee (HUAC), where he asserted
that there must be freedom for a creative writer to choose any topic and
to treat it in any style thought fit. He was asked to identify those who
had attended Communist Party meetings. He admitted attending the
meetings but he refused to name others who were present. He was given
a one-month suspended sentence for contempt of Congress and fined
$500. After an appeal to the Supreme Court, however, the conviction was
reversed. Nevertheless, audiences stopped coming to his plays and, for
nine years after *A View from the Bridge* (1955), no new play appeared on
the stage.

TopFoto

Arthur Miller and Marilyn Monroe in 1956

Miller had first met Marilyn Monroe in Hollywood in 1950, when she was a relatively unknown actress, and they had seen a lot of each other. When she came to New York in 1955 to study acting, they started dating and, in 1956 he divorced his wife and married Monroe. He looked after her career, rewriting her lines and interceding with directors, and he also tried to manage her intake of prescribed drugs and alcohol, and to boost her confidence. She suffered two failed pregnancies, however, and her health and her mental state deteriorated. Miller wrote the screenplay of *The Misfits* for her, but Monroe turned against Miller while they were working on the film, and they were divorced in 1961. She died from an overdose of barbiturates in August 1962. Critics interpret his play, *After the Fall* (1964) as, in part, an attempt to deal with this part of his life.

In spite of the HUAC, Miller continued to be politically active. He protested against the Vietnam War, saying that it was a 'criminal engagement which showed a side of American civilization I would rather

Taking it ▶
Further

Check out a fascinating documentary about Arthur Miller and Marilyn Monroe: go to www.youtube.com and search for 'Marilyn Monroe and Arthur Miller part one'.

not think about' (Bigsby). He covered the Nazi trials in Frankfurt for the *New York Herald Tribune*, and then wrote *Incident at Vichy*, a play about Nazism and anti-Semitism in Vichy France. He was a delegate to the National Democratic Party Convention in Chicago in 1968, and he worked for the anti-war movement. He was president of PEN, the international writers' organisation, for four years and protested against the oppression of writers worldwide.

In 1983 he directed *Death of a Salesman* in Beijing with a Chinese cast, an experience he wrote about in a book, illustrated with photographs by his third wife, Inge Morath. In 1984 he was awarded a lifetime achievement award. In 1987, his autobiography, *Timebends: A Life*, was published. He carried on writing plays until his death on 10 February, 2005, the fifty-sixth anniversary of *Salesman*'s opening night.

Historical context

The Industrial Revolution

Industrialisation brought prosperity for the nation, turning the USA into a great world power, and creating wealth for the few. Men such as John D. Rockefeller, the oil refiner, whose father was a travelling salesman, rose to control vast enterprises and make huge fortunes. Such successes fostered the dream that talent, determination and hard work were all that was needed to create immense personal wealth. Mechanisation, however, which we might have expected to bring progress and increased order, often had the reverse effect as the safety and welfare of the workers was neglected in the pursuit of high profits. The American economic system depends on persuading people that they need manufactured items so that they keep spending money, buying things, if necessary, on hire purchase. It is then all too easy to over-reach your budget by buying more than you can afford to repay.

The Great Depression

The Great Depression began in New York with the Wall Street Crash of October 1929, and rapidly spread worldwide. The stock market crash marked the beginning of a decade of high unemployment, poverty, low profits, deflation, plunging farm incomes, and lost opportunities for economic growth and personal advancement. Although its causes are still uncertain and controversial, the net effect was a sudden and general loss of confidence in the economic future.

Miller was just 14 when the stock market crashed, and the Depression hit his family very hard. Miller's father sold all his investments and even his insurance in order to keep his company out of bankruptcy, but to no avail. The family had to leave their comfortable apartment and move to a small house in Brooklyn which was, at the time, still semi-rural. The Depression had a profound effect on Miller. 'He learned that "there is a feeling at the back of the brain that the whole thing can sink at a moment's notice…everything else is ephemeral. It is going to blow away, except what a person is and what a relationship is"' (*The Cambridge Companion to Arthur Miller* edited by Christopher Bigsby, CUP, 1997, p. 1).

Willy Loman remembers that his best year was in 1928, the year before the stock market crash. Since then it has been a long struggle to make ends meet but he has weathered the years of the Depression and, ironically, Linda makes the last payment on the house on the day he commits suicide. It is because of the Depression that '*his exhaustion is apparent*', and that he has had to spend 'ten, twelve hours a day' trying to sell his wares (p. 28). The Depression is a significant contributory factor in his fate.

> **Context**
>
> Christopher Bigsby quotes Miller as saying in an interview that 'there were three suicides on the little block where we lived. They couldn't cope. The impact was incalculable. These people were profound believers in the American dream. The day the money stopped their identity was gone.'

Patriotism

Willy sincerely believes that the USA is 'the greatest country in the world' (p. 11). While at school he would have had to swear allegiance to the American flag regularly, and he would have been expected to learn by heart the speeches of great American statesmen. As a salesman, he would have thought of his travels as following in the footsteps of the pioneers, opening up new territories. He would have perceived selling as crucial to helping the economy expand and his country prosper. After the Depression and the Second World War, however, society's attitude was changing, and this helps to explain the controversy when *Death of a Salesman* opened on Broadway.

Social context

The play is firmly set in post-war New York by references to Ebbets Field, Hackensack and Brooklyn. American culture is suggested by

Taking it Further ▶

Read a traditional story about a yankee pedlar. Go to www.americanfolklore.net and search for 'Connecticut Yankee'.

Context

Two examples of salesmen who rose to the top are Edward Prizer, who became president of Vacuum Oil and Clarence Mott Woolley, who was president of the American Radiator Company.

Context

Miller wrote that travelling salesmen had 'a kind of intrepid valor that withstood the inevitable putdowns, the scoreless attempts to sell…These men lived…like actors whose product is first of all themselves, forever imagining triumphs in a world that either ignores them or denies their presence altogether. But just often enough to keep the game going one of them makes it and swings to the moon on a thread of dreams unwinding out of himself.' (*Timebends*, Methuen, 1987)

financial services such as mortgages, time payments and life insurance, as well as by brand names such as Chevrolet, Studebaker, Simonize, Hastings and General Electric, and by specific items such as aspirins and arch-supports.

In order to create markets for these goods, industries advertised widely and employed vast numbers of salesmen. Salesmen have always held a special place in American culture. There are many early tales about Yankee pedlars, marginal figures who operated at the fringes of established society, outwitting farmers and townspeople alike. In the twentieth century, salesmen, far from operating on the fringes of society, came to serve as embodiments of American capitalism.

In an interview with Laura Linard for Harvard Business School about his book *Birth of a Salesman* (2004), Walter A. Friedman says:

> **What made the US unique was the scale of American firms that were founded in the late nineteenth and early twentieth centuries. These massive manufacturing concerns, which produced tremendous numbers of business machines, appliances, and cars, hired salesmen in the hundreds in some cases, and even thousands in others, to create demand for their products. These goods, all pushed by aggressive salesmanship, distinguished the American economy by their early appearance and widespread purchase.**

In the 1930s, employers used to hold weekly meetings to boost the morale of their salesmen, at which they sang rousing songs such as 'Pack up your samples in your old black bag and sell, sell, sell!'

When Willy Loman chose selling in 1913, it was a career that had the potential to take him to the top of the firm because many of the powerful chief executives had spent part, or all, of their career in selling. However, the Depression created a different economic climate, and salesmen were very vulnerable to the downturn in the economy. By the time Arthur Miller wrote his play, the image of the salesman seemed to capture the entire tragedy of commercial society in the decades after depression and war. The play revealed the cruelty of a system of capitalism based on salesmanship, in which bosses fired people when they were no longer effective. Miller captures this disposability in a simple but memorable image when Willy tells his boss, 'You can't eat the orange and throw the peel away — a man is not a piece of fruit!' (p. 64).

Cultural context

Sport

At the beginning of the twentieth century, the development of radio and the technology to produce magazines and newspapers cheaply fuelled an obsession with spectator sports and the creation of sporting celebrities. American football has always been the most popular sport in the USA and, as well as professional leagues, high school and college leagues are still avidly followed. Matches are often played at top rank venues, such as Ebbets Field. Talented sportspeople are subjects of intense adulation, and it is possible to get scholarships to universities after graduation from high school on the strength of sporting prowess.

Athletic scholarships are a means by which universities can recruit players to their teams who otherwise might never be in a financial position to attend a university. The universities send out talent scouts like the three representatives who attend the Ebbets Field match. Willy boasts that Biff has scholarships to three universities, and Biff achieves the status of a young god when he becomes captain of the team. A crowd of girls follows him around and they even pay for him. His friends wait for him to give them orders such as 'Everybody sweep out the furnace room!'

The first great college player to move into the professional ranks in this era was the legendary Harold (Red) Grange (nicknamed 'the galloping ghost'), who, upon graduation from the University of Illinois, signed a contract with the Chicago Bears of the NFL in 1925. Grange played for Chicago for nine seasons and his presence in the league went a considerable distance to legitimising an organisation seen as distinctly second rate when compared to the college game.

Taking it ▶ Further

Check out archive footage of 'Red' Grange playing football. Search for 'Archival footage Red Grange' at www.youtube.com

Literary context

Greek drama

When Miller was asked which playwrights he most admired when he was young, his answer was 'Well, first the Greeks, for their magnificent form...That form has never left me; I suppose it just got burned in.' Greek tragedies are ritualistic enactments of the death of the spirit of the

old year and the birth of the new. It is possible to identify most of the elements from classical Greek tragedies in *Death of a Salesman*.

The *agon*, a struggle between winter and summer, is played out between Willy and Biff, and Willy's death is the *pathos*, the death of winter. It could be argued that Miller provides the *anagnorisis*, the discovery and recognition of the new spirit, in Willy's realisation that Biff loves him and has always loved him. This leads to the *peripeteia*, a quick turnaround in emotion from sorrow to joy: from accusing Biff of being a 'vengeful, spiteful mut', Willy, *'astonished, elevated'*, *'cries out his promise'*: 'That boy – that boy is going to be magnificent!' (pp. 105–06). The Requiem functions as the *threnos*, a lamentation for the dead spirit. Willy expected his death to be the *theophany*, the appearance of the new spirit in all his glory. He thinks that Biff, with the insurance money in his pocket, will be 'ahead of Bernard again' and, as he tells Ben, 'He'll worship me for it!' (p. 107). However, this is where Miller departs from his Greek model as the 'new spirit' declares that Willy had the wrong dreams and never knew who he was.

Early American writers

Benjamin Franklin advised that 'The Way to Wealth' was industry

One of the Founding Fathers, Benjamin Franklin, advised that 'The Way to Wealth' was industry. His vision was that, in the New World, every man is potentially a hero and that Christian values can lead the poorest of youths to become a successful man with a stake in society. Franklin advocated, 'industry and frugality, as the means of procuring wealth, and thereby securing virtue; it being more difficult for a man in want to act always honestly.' Under the pseudonym of Poor Richard, in a yearly almanac he wrote aphorisms such as 'Early to bed and early to rise, makes a Man healthy, wealthy and wise' and 'Industry pays debts'. These aphorisms falsely sold dreams of wealth made easily, just by leading a simple lifestyle.

A popular nineteenth-century novelist who fostered this vision of golden opportunities was the Reverend Horatio Alger. He wrote stories in which, through hard work, determination, courage, and concern for others, his characters achieved enough wealth and success to have a solid stake in society. Alger encouraged all men to believe that the American Dream was within their reach. However, many began to regard wealth as essential for the pursuit of happiness, which the Declaration of Independence had declared was an 'unalienable right'. Miller's play demonstrates the damaging effects of Alger's false promises and challenges the moral naivety of his books.

Ibsen

One of the strongest influences on Miller's work was Norwegian writer Henrik Ibsen, who was famous for writing about social issues in revolutionary ways. Ibsen's work examined the realities that lay behind many façades, revealing much that was disquieting to his contemporaries. Instead of being merely entertainment, Ibsen's plays challenged assumptions and directly addressed issues of morality. He wrote realistic tragedies about ordinary people who suffered fates they did not deserve, and he criticised society with an outspokenness that inspired Arthur Miller.

It was in Ibsen's plays that he found the retrospective structure in which an explosive situation in the present is both explained and brought to a crisis by the gradual revelation of the fatal secret, something that has happened in the past. In Ibsen's plays, and Miller's previous play *All My Sons*, the secret is a serious social crime that is publicly exposed, and the protagonist is forced to accept responsibility. In *Death of a Salesman*, however, there is no public exposure, no sudden shock revelation to the audience.

Miller reveals Willy's repressed memory in hints before it surfaces in Willy's mind. His guilt is not for a single act but for the realisation that he has not been a good husband and father. Throughout the play he is worried not only by his betrayal of Linda but also by the fear that he has taught his sons the wrong values and dreams. In his mind, his death is not an escape from the consequences of his guilt, as it is for Joe Keller in *All My Sons*, but a positive step towards building the American Dream for his son.

All My Sons was a conventionally realistic play but, for *Death of a Salesman*, Miller needed more freedom. He could not achieve the desired exploration of Willy's mind through realism alone. He used, like Tennessee Williams, a dramatic form that combined the illusion of objectivity afforded by Realism with the subjectivity of Expressionism.

Context

Arthur Miller adapted Ibsen's *An Enemy of the People* in the 1950s.

Context

Miller wrote:

…this play could not be encompassed by conventional realism, and for one integral reason: in Willy the past was as alive as what was happening at the moment, sometimes even crashing in to completely overwhelm his mind. I wanted precisely the same fluidity in the form, and now it was clear to me that this must be primarily verbal (*Timebends*).

Expressionism

The Expressionist movement arose in Germany at the beginning of the twentieth century in reaction to Realism. Expressionists were concerned with presenting the inner life of a character and how that character viewed the world rather than the objective representation favoured by Realists. They used symbols to evoke the unseen and the unconscious.

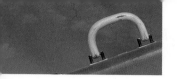

Miller's first image for *Death of a Salesman* was of 'an enormous face… which would appear and then open up, we would see the inside of a man's head'. In fact, *The Inside of His Head* was the first title. Willy's memories are an 'expression' of what is going on in Willy's mind, and Miller also uses lighting and music to suggest things of which Willy is not consciously aware.

He blends Expressionism and Realism to reflect the way the salesman's mind works. He creates a detailed and realistic impression of present time and then uses Expressionistic techniques to show how Willy Loman's mind wanders into the past and holds imaginary conversations with absent characters. Ben, at least, is not so much a character as a figment of Willy's imagination, conjured up by the memory of his one visit and distorted into the supportive confidant Willy needs. Miller does not use 'flashbacks' in the conventional sense but presents a subjective version of the past distorted by Willy's mind that overlaps with scenes in the present so that we can experience Willy's confusion.

The set blends sufficient realistic detail with an Expressionistic view of several rooms simultaneously and walls that can be ignored, helping to suggest that *'an air of the dream clings to the place, a dream rising out of reality'* (p. 7). Like Elizabethan theatres, the set needs a bare forestage where other scenes can be acted out with minimal props. Both music and lighting are used in an Expressionist way to help the audience feel for themselves what is going on inside Willy's head.

However, Miller does not use these techniques only to explore Willy's mind; he also uses them after Willy has died. The Requiem is also staged using Expressionist techniques. If these are used only to create a play that is seen from Willy's point of view, then this suggests that the Requiem is also presented as Willy might have seen it. Instead of watching objectively as family and friends mourn the inevitable death of a misguided man, the audience is still 'inside…his head' and subjectively sharing the poignancy of the final destruction of his dreams.

Tennessee Williams

While Miller was planning *Death of a Salesman*, he knew only one other writer with the same approach, Tennessee Williams. In *Timebends*, Miller writes that he could not imagine a theatre worth his time that did not want to change the world. He was impressed by how Williams had used a blend of Realism and Expressionism to create a unique feeling for his play. To express his universal truths and beliefs, Williams created what he termed 'plastic theatre' — a distinctive new style of drama. He insisted that all the elements of staging, including the set, lighting, music and sound effects, costumes and props, should work together to reflect and enhance the themes, characters, action and language.

When Miller watched *A Streetcar Named Desire* in December 1947, he wrote that it 'opened one specific door for me. Not the story or characters or the direction, but the words and their liberation, the joy of the writer in writing them, the radiant eloquence of its composition, moved me more than all its pathos' (*Timebends*). This inspired Miller to work even more precisely with Willy's use of language, realising that 'the language would of course have to be recognizably his to begin with, but it seemed possible now to infiltrate it with a kind of superconsciousness'.

Critical context

The original stage production of *Death of a Salesman* was greeted with excellent reviews by the press. Robert Garland, reviewer for the *New York Journal-American*, wrote that, on the first night, the audience was so emotionally shaken that people did not clap or move at the final curtain. Brooks Atkinson, reviewer for the *New York Times*, wrote:

> **Miller has written a superb drama…It is so simple in style and so inevitable in theme that it scarcely seems like a thing that has been written and acted. For Mr Miller has looked with compassion into the hearts of ordinary Americans and quietly transferred their hope and anguish to the theatre. (1949)**

For the early reviewers, the main theme was the gap between Willy's illusions and his reality, and they saw his inability to reconcile them as the primary cause of his suicide.

Capitalist criticism

As a piece of theatre it was a resounding success, but some reviewers criticised Miller for his anti-capitalist stance. The HUAC (see p. 66 of this guide) was beginning its investigations, and criticism of American business practices was viewed as unpatriotic. Eleanor Clark, in *Partisan Review*, wrote that, for Miller:

Context

Robert Garland wrote that Miller 'asked — demanded, rather — your sympathy as a fellow member of the bedevilled human race and your attention as an intelligent collaborator as well' (*New York Journal-American*, 1949).

Context

Brooks Atkinson wrote that *Salesman* was 'One of the finest dramas in the whole range of American theatre' (*New York Times,* 1949).

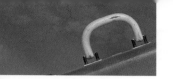

it is, of course, the capitalist system that has done Willy in; the scene in which he is brutally fired after some forty years with the firm comes straight from [Communist] party line literature of the 'thirties; and the idea emerges lucidly enough through all the confused motivations of the play that it is our particular form of money economy that has bred the absurdly false ideals of both father and sons.

This view was refuted by Brian Clark in his essay 'Point of View in Arthur Miller's *Death of a Salesman*' (1966). He pointed out that, in the first place, 'Willy's employer, Howard, is not presented as a conscious monster, but as a man very like Willy himself'; 'Secondly, Willy's plight is shewn to be at least partly the result of his own character', and 'Thirdly, the play balances the failure of Willy and his children with the success of Charley and his son'.

Marxist criticism

The Marxist perspective is that works of literature are conditioned by the economic and political forces of their social context. Marxist critics view the play as a critique of a capitalist society that degrades the unsuccessful. As a salesman, Willy knows that it is personality that makes sales, and he has had to sell himself in order to make a living. Ultimately, he reduces himself to a commodity and sells his own life for the insurance payment. However, close analysis of the characters of Charley and Howard Wagner makes it difficult to read the play as a piece of Marxist propaganda, especially since Charley offers Willy another opportunity to make a living in the capitalist system.

Psychoanalytic criticism

Psychoanalytic critics see literature as similar to dreams. Both are fictions, inventions of the mind that, although based on reality, are, by definition, not literally true. The theory is that much of what lies in the unconscious mind has been repressed, or censored, by consciousness and emerges only in disguised forms such as dreams.

Dr Daniel E. Schneider says that Willy's 'past as in hallucination, comes back to him; not chronologically as in a flashback, but *dynamically with the logic of his erupting volcanic unconscious*. In psychiatry we call this "the return of the repressed"' (*The Psychoanalyst and the Artist*, 1950). He reads the play as a version of the Oedipus myth: both Willy and Happy are unhappy younger brothers, seeking to surpass, perhaps replace, their siblings, and Happy is trying to 'come out number-one man' in his father's place.

Linguistic criticism

The play has also been criticised for being 'written as solid, sometimes stolid prose. To its credit, it has no fake poetry, but it has no real poetry either' (*Time* magazine, 1949). Joseph Wood Krutch described the language of the play as 'prosy and pedestrian', 'undistinguished', 'unpoetic', 'unmemorable', and 'unquotable' (*The Nation*). Stanley Kauffmann wrote that 'often the dialogue slips into a fanciness that is slightly ludicrous. To hear Biff say, "I've been remiss," or to hear Linda say, "He was crestfallen, Willy," is like watching a car run off the road momentarily onto the shoulder' (*The New Republic, 1976*).

Other critics, however, have praised Miller's use of language. In 1979, Dennis Welland wrote that Miller's 'practice has usually been to lift the dialogue fractionally above the incoherencies of everyday intercourse while keeping it firmly grounded in the rhythm of ordinary speech and the **idiom** of the **vernacular**'. Brian Parker wrote that, 'The language… is an accurate record of the groping half-inarticulate, cliché-ridden inadequacy of ordinary American speech.' When the Lomans use more elevated language, it serves to indicate their ambition to be something more than those who are, to quote Biff's phrase, 'a dime a dozen'.

Some critics point to the influences of Yiddish, a High German language of Ashkenazi Jewish origin, which was spoken by Miller's family. In a review of a production of a Yiddish translation, George Ross claimed that 'this Yiddish production is really the original, and the Broadway production was merely Arthur Miller's translation into English' (1951). David Mamet, the playwright, said of *Salesman* that:

> **the greatest American play, arguably, is the story of a Jew told by a Jew and cast in 'universal' terms. Willy Loman is a Jew in a Jewish industry, but he is never identified as such. His story is never avowed as a Jewish story, and so a great contribution to Jewish American history is lost. (1998)**

However, Dennis Welland has pointed out that 'A markedly Jewish Willy Loman might have made the play seem an overt attack on covert anti-Semitism in American business. By making Willy ethnically neutral Miller emphasises his point that Willy's trouble is that he is Willy in a particular society.'

vernacular the oral variety of language belonging to a particular community

idiom a way of expressing oneself which cannot be translated into another language because its meaning is not equivalent to the arrangement of words used

Context

In a review of a production by Traveling Jewish Theater on **www.jweekly.com**, Corey Fischer, the actor who played Willy, says, 'I'm finding Willy's language just flows right into a New York Jewish intonation…sometimes it's an intangible speech rhythm.'

Taking it Further

Watch Lee J. Cobb as Willy Loman in 1966: go to www.youtube.com/ and search for 'Cobb Willy Loman'

It is interesting that, although Miller never accepted that Willy Loman was a Jewish role, his three favourite actors who played the character were all Jewish. Lee J. Cobb played Willy in the original Broadway production and, although he was much larger than Miller intended, he had a gentle humanity that Miller felt suited the part, and his size somehow made Willy's suicide seem more tragic. In fact *The New York Post* review criticised this, saying that, 'Willy Loman assumes a personal force that keeps him from being quite the pathetic failure the author made him' (1949). The other actors who impressed Miller were Warren Mitchell and Dustin Hoffman.

Feminist criticism

Kay Stanton is outspoken in her criticism of what she calls the 'male American Dream', which is:

> **as the play shows, unbalanced, immature, illogical, lying, thieving, self-contradictory, and self-destructive. Only Willy literally kills himself, but the Dream's celebration of the masculine mythos is inherently self-destructive in its need to obliterate other men…It prefers to destroy itself rather than to acknowledge the female as equal or to submit to a realistic and balanced feminine value system… ('Women and the American Dream of *Death of a Salesman*', 1989)**

Linda Kintz writes that:

> **Miller's play simultaneously critiques the restriction and damage perpetrated by the rigid gender roles of this oedipal model of family with the white male as head and longs for the imagined stability of a time in a mythical American past when men could unproblematically own their plot of ground and plant it, wives were always available, and men really were the head of the family. ('The Sociosymbolic Work of Family in *Death of a Salesman*', 1995)**

Taking it Further

If the harsh treatment of women in America in the 1940s is a theme that interests you, you might like to read the play or watch the film of *A Streetcar named Desire* by Tennessee Williams.

Happy is insulting towards women, dehumanising them as 'creatures', 'pig' and 'strudel', and he draws attention to Miss Forsyth's 'binoculars', a slang term for breasts. He uses and abuses women, as Biff used to when he was a popular schoolboy. Feminists have complained that the marginalisation of women and Linda's self-effacing role date the play and diminish its status, but the play is firmly set in post-war New York, and so Miller had to reflect the subordination of women in post-war culture. However, in Linda he has created a strong woman who is arguably the real hero. She has moral integrity, self-sacrificing love and a magnificent dignity that cannot help but arouse admiration, even if the audience criticises her for fostering Willy's dreams.

Working with the text

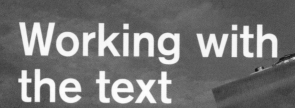

Meeting the Assessment Objectives

The Assessment Objectives (AOs) describe the skills you must demonstrate to get a good grade.

AO1: Articulate, creative, informed and relevant responses to literary texts, using appropriate terminology and concepts, and coherent, accurate written expression.

For AO1, you need to write fluently, structuring your essay, guiding your reader through your line of argument and using the vocabulary, including critical terminology, appropriate to an A-level essay. You need to use frequent embedded quotations to give evidence of close detailed knowledge, and you should demonstrate familiarity with the whole text.

AO2: Demonstrate detailed critical understanding in analysing the ways in which structure, form and language shape meaning in literary texts.

To improve your marks for AO2, it is a good idea to practise writing in **analytical sentences**.

AO3i: Explore connections and comparisons between different literary texts.

Your examination board may require you to compare and contrast one or more other texts with *Death of a Salesman*, and you should try to find specific points of comparison, rather than merely generalising. If this AO is assessed in single-text questions, you could explore how Miller's style developed from his earlier play *All My Sons*, or consider another text criticising the American Dream, such as Sinclair Lewis's satire, *Babbitt*, or Scott Fitzgerald's *The Great Gatsby*.

AO3ii: Look at various possible different interpretations and use these to develop your own.

---

analytical sentences

- a brief quotation or close reference
- a definition or description of the feature you intend to analyse
- an explanation of how Miller has used this feature
- an evaluation of what Miller has achieved by using it

…we cannot know what is factual and what is imagined or exaggerated

---

PHILIP ALLAN LITERATURE GUIDE **FOR A-LEVEL**

This implies looking at various critical views as well as thinking about what your fellow students and you yourself think. Because the play explores events and characters from Willy's point of view, we cannot know what is factual and what is imagined or exaggerated, so there are plenty of opportunities for you to explore different presentations of characters and interpretations of events.

AO4: Demonstrate understanding of the significance and influence of the contexts in which literary texts are written and received.

Some awareness of the effect of the Wall Street Crash and the Depression on the American economy and the American psyche is essential here. You should also demonstrate understanding of the historical roots of the American Dream. The most significant literary influences on Miller are Greek drama, Henrik Ibsen, Expressionism and Tennessee Williams.

Taking it **Further** ➤

There is a Philip Allan Literature Guide in this series for Tennessee Williams's *A Streetcar named Desire*, which you would find very helpful for a comparative study with *Death of a Salesman*.

Essay writing

The following sections give guidance on writing essays. Sample essays at A and C grades are provided online in the Downloads section of the free website at **www.philipallan.co.uk/literatureguidesonline**.

Extract-based essay questions

Here are the questions to address when analysing drama text passages:

- Is it set in social time, psychic time or both?
- Why has Miller included this scene in the play? What is its importance?
- How does this scene fit into the narrative structure of the play?
- Which of the themes is Miller evoking here, and how does this scene fit into his treatment of that theme in the whole play?
- What previous scenes do we need to recall in order to understand the implications of this scene?
- Does this extract foreshadow any future scenes?
- Does Miller use any recurring images or symbols in this passage? If so, analyse how they fit into the overall pattern.
- If there are stage directions, what mood is Miller evoking and how does he do it?
- What do the spoken language features tell us about each speaker?
- Are there any words, phrases or metaphors that would reward close analysis? Why has Miller included them?

Whole-text questions

Make sure you know which Assessment Objectives are examined by your board and concentrate on those. AO1 is assessed by looking at your whole essay and judging whether your writing skills and vocabulary are appropriate for A-level, whether your essay has been carefully planned and whether you are clearly very familiar with the whole text. The other Assessment Objectives you can plan for (see p. 80 of this guide).

Sample question

Many definitions of tragedy claim that at the end of the play positives have emerged. Is it possible to see anything positive in the ending of *Death of a Salesman*?

Possible approach

- This question has probably been set to enable you to consider whether or not this play can be called a tragedy, but at the beginning of your essay you should directly address the question. You may think that the most positive element to have emerged at the end is the strength of the family ties, or you may be of the opinion that it is the fact that Charley, a successful businessman, understands Willy's predicament and demonstrates the benevolent face of capitalism.

- You can meet the requirements of AO2 'form' by analysing stage directions, and 'structure' by exploring Miller's use of the classical elements of tragedy (see pp. 56–57 of this guide). You could argue that, although there is no **theophany**, the audience is reassured that it is possible to achieve the American Dream, as long as your expectations are realistic.

- When tragic heroes die, the audience feels that their deaths are a waste of potentially worthwhile lives, and you can explore the 'language' of Linda's eloquent speeches for AO2 to demonstrate that, for her at least, Willy's death is a tragedy, and the positive element is that he is remembered for what he did achieve.

- There is an opportunity to gain marks for AO3 by offering alternative interpretations. The ending could be regarded as positive because Willy dies happy, thinking that Biff will worship him for enabling him to inherit the insurance money and that hundreds of people will come to his funeral. On the other hand, the Requiem demonstrates that his death achieves neither of these objectives.

- You can cover AO4 by exploring the effects of the Great Depression and the theme of the American Dream.

- You could conclude your line of argument by saying that, whether or not the protagonist is 'a small man' or 'a great man', a play can be

theophany the appearance of the new spirit in all his glory in Greek drama

defined as a tragedy if it is felt at the end that his death was a waste. Willy's death was wasted because, in spite of his sense of failure, he had achieved the American Dream. He and Linda had paid off the house and brought up two sons who were earning their own living. They could have sold their house and retired to a 'little place out in the country' where they could have been self-sufficient. Although Willy brought about his own fate, he was a victim of the false interpretation of the Dream.

...a play can be defined as a tragedy if it is felt at the end that his death was a waste

Comparative questions

The examiners may expect you to offer a balanced essay, or they may set this play as a core text to be compared with one carrying less weight. As always, AO1 will be assessed throughout but you can plan carefully to meet the requirements of the other AOs.

Sample question

How do you respond to the claim that *Death of a Salesman* is a story about reality and illusion?

Possible approach comparing *Death of a Salesman* with Tennessee Williams's *The Glass Menagerie*

- It is especially important in a comparative essay to decide on your line of argument before you start planning your essay. In Williams's play, each member of the Wingfield family has difficulty accepting and relating to reality, and each, as a result, withdraws into a private world of illusion.

- Willy Loman and his sons have the same difficulty, but Linda has her feet firmly on the ground.

- For AO2 analysis of 'form', you should explore the dramatic techniques of the two playwrights, both of whom blend an expressionistic set with lighting, symbols and sound effects. Both plays feature sets where apartment buildings surround the protagonists and the characters walk through walls into memories of the past, and both playwrights have used **leitmotifs** and suggested individual melodies to be associated with particular characters.

leitmotif a frequently repeated phrase, image or symbol in a literary work, the recurrence of which supports a theme

- For AO2 analysis of 'structure', you could explore the ways in which Tom Wingfield's past, like Willy's, intrudes into his present, but contrast Williams's use of an involved narrator with Miller's methods of exploring the inside of Willy's head.

- For AO2 analysis of 'language', you could also gain marks for AO4 by pointing out that Miller was inspired by Williams's use of 'words and their liberation, the joy of the writer in writing them, the radiant

Tom and Biff...
are both trapped:
both physically
leave but are
unable to cut
themselves
off from their
families.

eloquence of its composition'. Whereas Miller captures the lower-middle-class speech of not very well educated people in Brooklyn, Tom is a poet and the play is set in St Louis, so the illusions and the language are different.

- For AO3, you could explore the significance of the abandonment of both Tom and Willy by their fathers. You could also explore the similarity between Tom and Biff, who are both trapped: both physically leave but are unable to cut themselves off from their families.

- For AO4, you should explore the effects of the Great Depression and an understanding of the historical roots of the American Dream.

Transformational writing

Sample task

Write a re-creative piece for the play in which Happy tries to explain to Charley why he denied his father and walked out of the restaurant. Try to build upon Miller's presentation of his character and echo specific aspects of his form, structure and language. Write a brief commentary to accompany your new text which explains how and where you have tried to reflect the original play.

Extract from answer

CHARLEY: How couldya do it to him, Happy? How couldya?

HAPPY: I tried, Charley; you know I did. I sent Mom and Pop to Florida on vacation. I gave them a few dollars sometimes 'cause I know it's been hard for Pop to sell much since the Crash. I took Pop into town. It was *me* not Biff that went down in the middle of the night to try and cheer Pop up, but Mom calls *me* 'a philandering bum'. Can you credit it? Whatever I did for them it weren't enough. Biff'd come home once a year — he brought 'em nothin', but he was the only one they had eyes for. Pop was talking to Biff most of the time even when he weren't there, and Mom ignored me. She even ignored me when I told her I was gettin' married. I knew Pop had no pension, but I had no idea that he was working only on commission. You could've knocked me down with a feather when Mom told us. Pop was always tellin' everyone how successful he was — how was I supposed to know? Then Mom blamed me for not giving him more. It just ain't fair.

CHARLEY: I know, Hap, but to abandon him like that...!

HAPPY: It was real embarrassing. He was arguin' with Biff, and then he suddenly hit him. Right in the face. I tried to get the two of them to behave proper, and then Biff took out the rubber tube and accused *me* of not caring. He had the gall to turn round and say 'you don't give a good goddam about him'! Suddenly I realised that I was wasting my time. I thought 'What's the point?' Whatever I do it ain't right, it ain't good enough. Nobody realises how I've tried to help. Pop always only wanted Biff, and Mom was so worried about Pop that she didn't appreciate anything I did. She still thought of me as the baby. As usual, Biff ran away, leaving me to look after Pop, and I thought, 'Hell, no! I'm not picking up the pieces for him any more!' If he can walk out then so can I.

Student's own commentary

I have built on Miller's presentation of Happy as the undervalued son, referring to things he had done for his parents and their lack of appreciation. I have used the spoken language features that Miller does, including repetition, clichés (knocked me down with a feather), swearing (Hell), elision (couldya), incomplete sentences (Right in the face.) and also **aposiopesis** (to abandon him like that…) to indicate Charley's shock. I have tried to use uneducated American syntax, such as the adjectives 'real' and 'proper' instead of the adverbial form, and the plural verb with a singular subject in 'he weren't there', as well as the Americanisms 'dollars', 'vacation', 'ain't' and 'Mom' and 'Pop'.

aposiopesis when a dramatist deliberately makes a character break off in mid-sentence.

Examiner's comments

AO1 — quality of writing:

- Appropriate spelling, punctuation and grammar
- Vocabulary appropriate to an uneducated New Yorker of the 1940s
- A creative and original point of view, looking at matters from Happy's perspective
- Creating and sustaining a believable register
- Varied sentence structure that reflects source text
- No unnecessary narration/storytelling/plot recount

AO2 — form, structure and language:

- Sense that the language used is a 'map of the character's mind'
- Sense that the character chosen is understood and the attitudes he displays are convincing and likely, based on a close reading of the text
- Use of figurative language in clichés
- Implied understanding of the symbolism of the rubber tube

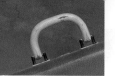

Task 12

Write a re-creative piece describing the incident in Boston from the Woman's point of view. What story would she have to tell about her affair with Willy Loman and the way it came to an end? Write a brief commentary to accompany your new text explaining how you have tried to reflect the original play.

- Specific reflections of Miller's text that show a seamless overarching understanding

AO3 — different interpretations:

- Offers a different interpretation of Happy instead of merely seeing him as shallow and uncaring

AO4 — contexts:

- References and speech appropriate to the era in which the text is set
- Clear reference to the Wall Street Crash and the fact that few private companies had pension schemes in the 1940s

Extended commentaries

1 Linda rebukes her sons (pp. 44–45)

In this speech, Miller not only reveals more about Willy's state of mind, he substantially raises Linda's profile in the play. In response to Biff's attack on Willy's employers, she demands that he search his own conscience with the rhetorical question, 'Are they any worse than his sons?' Her language is straightforward, but she speaks with an unadorned eloquence that is arguably the most persuasive form of rhetoric.

She evokes the past with positive associations, using words such as 'young', 'glad', 'friends' and 'loved', then she juxtaposes them with the present using words with negative associations such as 'dead' and 'exhausted'. She speaks lyrically but without using any self-conscious poetic devices. The simple **syndetic listing** of 'takes the valises out of the car and puts them back and takes them out again and he's exhausted' rhythmically evokes the repetitive hopelessness of what Willy's life has been reduced to. She caps this with the internal rhyming in 'Instead of walking he talks now.'

syndetic listing
when a writer puts a conjunction between each of the elements in the list instead of using commas

Repetition of 'no one' drives home the loneliness, and then she gives voice to a relentless barrage of eleven questions, trying to force her sons to empathise with their father. When she asks for a second time how long Willy can go on borrowing money from Charley, it becomes obvious that what she is 'sitting here and waiting for' is Willy's death, because what other outcome could there be if her sons do not do anything? Underlying this speech is the painful knowledge that her love is not enough to save Willy. She has done everything she can. Her tone is one of desperation: if she cannot persuade Biff that his father's life is worth saving, then Willy will die.

As the speech gathers pace, her tone becomes more urgent, and she drives home her points by repeating the interrogatives 'Why?' and 'How long?' When Happy interrupts, she dismisses his objection but she is not thrown off course. She turns to Biff and appeals to his memories of the past. She has succeeded in making him agree to stay, but that is not what she wants — his presence provokes Willy. What she has been pushing for is that Biff should agree to give his father emotional support. She has to resort to revealing the details about Willy's attempts on his life and, eventually, when '*she is bent over in the chair, weeping, her face in her hands*', Biff succumbs to her persuasion and kneels in front of her in an attitude of submission.

2 Requiem: Charley's speech (p. 111)

Being a businessman who employs salesmen, Charley knows the pressures of the job, telling Willy: 'My New England man comes back and he's bleedin', they murdered him up there' (p. 40). Charley has offered Willy another chance to earn his living, but Willy has been unable to let go of his dreams and in this speech we learn that Charley understands.

Charley opens his speech with an ultimatum in universal terms. 'Nobody' is a negative generic pronoun that embraces the characters in the play, the audience and society as a whole. Miller gives Charley the archaic mandative **subjunctive** form of the verb 'dare' as he delivers his command to society that nobody must blame Willy for what he has done. Charley sounds like Miller's mouthpiece as he explains the difficulties of a salesman's life in simple concrete images.

subjunctive the form of a verb that expresses uncertainty or non-factuality, for example, 'If I were you'.

A house built with a 'rock bottom' is solid, but there is no firm foundation to a salesman's life as there is to that of someone who earns his living with specialist knowledge or skills. A salesman is like a sailor 'way out there in the blue' at the mercy of the winds of fortune. The only tools he has to work with, 'a smile and a shoeshine', are insubstantial and, once he is unable to sell himself, nobody will buy from him any more. In an elemental metaphor, Charley compares the time when the buyers stop smiling back to an earthquake, because this is the time when everything he has worked for is destroyed.

Charley then repeats his imperative and follows it with two simple sentences, pointing out that a salesman has got to dream because his livelihood depends on his believing that he will be successful. Miller's use of colloquial dialect forms of verbs ('he don't' and 'A salesman is got to dream') in Charley's speech makes him sound less like a Chorus and reminds the audience that Charley is a self-made man.

Top ten quotations

1

...we see a solid vault of apartment houses around the small fragile-seeming home. (p. 7)

It is always profitable to analyse Miller's stage directions. Here he evokes an arched structure forming a roof above the house with the use of the word 'vault'. He wants the set to convey Willy's feeling of being 'boxed' in, even if it is not realistic. In contrast to the *'towering angular shapes'* that oppress the scenes in present time, the house is small and seems fragile. Significantly, Miller calls it a 'home', suggesting that the building is a metaphor for the fragile family structure.

2

The world is an oyster, but you don't crack it open on a mattress! (Willy, p. 32)

Miller ironically gives Willy a quotation from Pistol, Shakespeare's notorious thief, 'the world's mine oyster'. Pistol declared that, since Falstaff would not lend him a penny, he would look elsewhere. Just as an oyster will yield a pearl to the man who can force it open, the whole world will yield riches to a ruthless man with a sword. However, Willy does not have enough education to understand Shakespeare's meaning. He takes it to mean that dreams can come true, that the world is Happy's for the taking. However, he adds a proviso, warning that Happy needs to be aggressive to achieve it — he will not be able to reach the pearl if he tries to open the oyster with a soft object like a mattress. Of course, there is also the suggestion that Happy cannot get to the top of his profession by sleeping with women, even if they are the fiancées of executives.

> **Taking it Further**
>
> You may like to explore the original context for the quotation in Shakespeare's *The Merry Wives of Windsor* (II.2.3).

3

William, when I walked into the jungle, I was seventeen. When I walked out I was twenty-one. And, by God, I was rich! (Ben, pp. 40–41)

Willy remembers and keeps repeating the words of Ben's declaration in a different order. He has memorised it and it has become a kind of

mantra for him, a philosophy that he hopes will transform the lives of his sons. The verb 'walk' suggests that the riches came without effort, all that was needed was the courage to go into a hostile environment, but four years' working in diamond mines cannot have been easy.

mantra a phrase that resonates for you, suggesting a way to live

---

Attention, attention must be finally paid to such a person. (Linda, p. 44)

4

In this speech of Linda's, Miller juxtaposes a simple monosyllabic concrete image of a man falling 'into his grave like an old dog' with this formal-sounding passive construction. Rather than use the personal active voice in 'You must pay attention', Miller has foregrounded the abstract noun 'attention', which is repeated for emphasis. Miller has omitted the agentive phrase so that the declaration can be interpreted as an imperative directed at society as a whole. The adverbial 'finally' also achieves extra emphasis by being embedded within the verb phrase. Linda has become Miller's mouthpiece, speaking not only to her sons but also conveying Miller's message to society.

A star like that, magnificent, can never really fade away! (Willy, p. 54)

5

Just as a star shines brightly against the dark sky, so glamorous celebrities are said to shine, particularly in the worlds of entertainment and sport, giving lesser mortals something spectacular to look up to and wonder at. Willy imagines Biff to be no ordinary star, however: he is 'magnificent', a Latinate word that means that he does great things. Miller gives this adjective extra emphasis by placing it in parenthesis instead of before the noun. The pauses have the effect of making Willy sound in awe of Biff, continuing the association of him with Hercules. To Willy, the Ebbets Field game was much more than a mere high-school football match. It was the occasion where the young god proved his immortality to the world and, crucial to the memory, waved to Willy in front of everyone.

The only thing you got in this world is what you can sell. (Charley, pp. 76–77)

6

This monosyllabic statement by Charley sums up the cynical opposing viewpoint to Willy's obsession with being well-liked. We know that this is not Charley's philosophy because he has been lending Willy money, with no hope of repayment, and he offers Willy a job, knowing that Willy is exhausted and no longer able to work effectively. Charley is still trying to puncture Willy's dreams and keep him in touch with reality.

7

> **Funny, y'know? After all the highways, and the trains, and the appointments, and the years, you end up worth more dead than alive. (Willy, p. 77)**

'Funny' is a colloquial expression that acknowledges Willy's understanding of the irony of his situation. Miller gives Willy a syndetic list to emphasise his exhaustion with travelling, but to the rhetorical triplet he adds a fourth. Willy thinks of 'the years' as one long struggle and, in his estimation, he has achieved nothing because he measures a man's 'worth' in the amount of money he leaves behind.

8

> **...the woods are burning, boys, you understand? There's a big blaze going on all around. I was fired today. (Willy, p. 84)**

Biff speaks '*with determination*', forcing Willy to listen, but his father gets angry and says that 'the woods are burning' to suggest how he feels. This is an important metaphor for understanding the inside of Willy's head. A forest fire soon gets out of control and threatens to destroy everything in its path. There is nothing its victims can do to quench the flames, and the smoke distorts their vision. Willy feels beset on all sides by things beyond his control and he can see no way out of his situation. This is a cry for help because he can no longer cope with life. We know that he is contemplating suicide, a frightening solution that he has already attempted several times. His last hope is that Biff has good news.

9

> **A man can't go out the way he came in, Ben, a man has got to add up to something. You can't, you can't — (Willy, p. 99)**

This quotation sums up Willy's dream. He has been struggling all his life to leave something behind him. What he wanted was to create a business to pass on to his sons. Since he has not done that, he plans to leave his life insurance money. This is the dream he tried to pass on to Biff, but Biff is more content to live from day to day. Willy's insistence that he should make something of himself goes against Biff's nature and causes the tension between them. Once again, Miller gives Willy a metaphor from the semantic field of finance: he needs to 'add up' to something, but he is just 'ringing up a zero' on the cash register of life (p. 100). The aposiopesis at the end of this quotation suggests that he is hesitant and perhaps is beginning to realise that his dream is wrong, but he hangs on to it with Ben to support him in his imagination.

Time, William, time!...The boat. We'll be late. (Ben, pp. 107–08)

In Willy's mind, Ben has always been in a hurry and here Willy imagines Ben urging Willy to come with him. Now, for Willy, time is running out. The jungle of life that offered such potential success has become a forest fire threatening to overwhelm him. The only way out that he can see is death, and Ben has come back from the dead to collect him. With a reference to classical mythology and the ferry boat across the River Styx into the underworld, Miller shows that Willy perceives death as a positive move. The first person plural pronoun 'we' shows that Willy believes that he has company on his journey, but the Ben he has conjured up in his imagination moves away unnoticed, and, when he realises he is alone, Willy utters a gasp of fear.

Taking it further

Websites

- **www.ibiblio.org/miller/** is the official website of the Arthur Miller Society with useful links to other sites related to Miller and his contemporaries.
- **www.teachervision.fen.com** has a resource pack of questions, exercises and assignments published by Walden University. Search for *Death of a Salesman* or go to **http://tinyurl.com/39znj2r**.

Films

- **1951:** directed by Laslo Benedek and starring Fredric March. Not readily available.
- **1966:** directed by Alex Segal and starring Lee J. Cobb. This is a film of the 1966 Broadway production. There are some annoying cuts of significant details, but Cobb has a beautifully expressive face and is a sympathetic Willy.
- **1985:** directed by Volker Schlöndorff and starring Dustin Hoffman. This film is faithful to the text and Hoffman is totally convincing, filled with nervous energy, mercurial, volatile and yet vulnerable.

Taking it ►
Further ►

Look at this poster for the film starring Fredric March www.lovingtheclassics. com/deathofasalesman. jpg. Note which themes it thinks are most important and then design your own poster.

Taking it ►
Further ►

Watch a short excerpt from this film. Go to http://video. google.com and search for 'Salesman Cobb'.

Television

- **1996:** directed by David Thacker and starring Warren Mitchell. A few scenes from this production are available on the internet and well worth watching. Go to **www.youtube.com** and search for 'Warren Mitchell as Willy'.
- **2000:** directed by Kirk Browning and starring Brian Dennehy.

Biographies

- Miller, A. (1983) *Salesman in Beijing,* Methuen
- Miller, A. (1987) *Timebends: A Life,* Methuen
  - Miller's autobiography makes fascinating reading and he makes some significant comments on *Death of a Salesman.*

Criticism

- Bigsby, C. (ed.) (1997) *The Cambridge Companion to Arthur Miller,* CUP
  - Includes an interesting introduction by Bigsby and an excellent essay by Matthew C. Roudané about '*Death of a Salesman* and the poetics of Arthur Miller'.
- Bloom, H. (ed.) (1988) *Arthur Miller's Death of a Salesman,* Bloom's Modern Critical Interpretations Series, Chelsea House Publications
  - A collection of excellent essays written between 1963 and 1984.